The Guardian

Kent Long

LifeRich Publishing is a registered trademark of The Reader's Digest Association, Inc.

LifeRich Publishing books may be ordered through booksellers or by contacting:

LifeRich Publishing
1663 Liberty Drive
Bloomington, IN 47403
www.liferichpublishing.com
844-686-9607

Scripture taken from the New King James Version. Copyright © 1979, 1980, 1982 by Thomas Nel-son, Inc. Used by permission. All rights reserved.

ISBN: 978-1-4897-3210-1 (sc)
ISBN: 978-1-4897-3211-8 (hc)
ISBN: 978-1-4897-3219-4 (e)

Library of Congress Control Number: 2020923358

Print information available on the last page.

LifeRich Publishing rev. date: 11/18/2020

ROMANS 13:4

FOR HE IS GOD'S MINISTER TO YOUR FOR GOOD. BUT IF YOU DO EVIL, BE AFRAID; FOR HE DOES NOT BEAR THE SWORD IN VAIN; FOR HE IS GOD'S MINISTER, AN AVENGER TO EXECUTE WRATH ON HIM WHO PRACTICES EVIL.

PSALMS 144 1:1-2

1. Blessed be the LORD my strength which teacheth my hands to war, and my fingers to fight:
2. My goodness, and my fortress; my high tower, and my deliverer; my shield, and he in whom I trust...

CHAPTER ONE

IT WAS MID-APRIL AND STILL cool in the mornings when Jeremiah Edwin Dyson came in from his morning stroll at the Blue Cedar Retirement Home in Phoenix. Today had started out like most every day. Jerimiah (J.E.D. to everyone who knew him or knew of him) started his day with a devotion and a stroll so he could talk to his Lord. But today was different—he was to meet his new great-grandson.

Now, J.E.D. had just turned 100 years old on April 2 and although there had been quite a celebration, what thrilled him the most was that this great-grandson was born on his birthday. J.E.D. was getting more anxious by the minute waiting for his arrival.

At about 8:15 a.m., J.E.D. was in his favorite chair, reading, when he heard a few light taps on the door. He said, "Come in this house," putting the Bible down as he got to his feet.

Frank Taylor, J.E.D.'s grandson-in-law, stuck his head in the room and said, "Are you ready to meet your great-grandson?" J.E.D. replied, "Oh, yeah," as he made his way to the door, grinning from ear to ear.

When Sabrina, J.E.D.'s granddaughter, walked through the door with the baby boy she could see that Grandpa J.E.D. was about to cry because of the joy of this moment.

The tears welling up in his eyes as he reached and touched the baby boy's head, J.E.D. said to the baby, "*Osiyo, chooch,*" an affectionate Cherokee hello. J.E.D. raised his hand toward heaven with tears of joy in his eyes. All he could say was, "Thank you Jesus, thank you Jesus." This was the moment he had been waiting for since he heard that Sabrina was going to have a baby. Somehow this had taken J.E.D. back many years.

J.E.D. only had one child, Colette, a beautiful girl with gray-blue eyes that people couldn't keep from looking at and wavy hair that reminded you of a child movie star. Her features, from her eyebrows to her cheeks, nose, lips and chin, looked like they came from a wish list. J.E.D. had been blessed with Colette.

J.E.D. had also been blessed with a gorgeous wife, Kenna. She was a lovely, petite lady with dark brown hair, dark eyes and features that looked like they came from a porcelain doll. Sabrina looked so much like Kenna.

The good Lord had taken a child away from J.E.D. and Kenna before it was born and although he never felt any bitterness, J.E.D. had felt like there was something missing from that moment on.

Until now. There was the face he had seen many years ago. This baby looked just like Colette. There were those same perfect nose and lips, eyes and, yeah, these looks run in the family. At this moment, the feeling that something had been missing vanished.

After hugs to Frank and Sabrina and a kiss to the baby, J.E.D. sat back down in his chair and asked Sabrina to bring the baby to him.

The baby had just begun to get a little fussy when J.E.D. began to talk to him. To Frank and Sabrina's amazement, the baby calmed down and appeared to be almost mesmerized by his great grandpa.

As J.E.D. held the baby, he asked Frank and Sabrina the baby's name. Sabrina said with a smile, "It's a special name to Frank and me and we hope you're pleased with it, it's Jeremiah Edwin Taylor—J.E.T.!"

Sabrina didn't think she could see her grandpa be any prouder than he already was, but she was wrong. J.E.D. said, "Pleased? I couldn't be more grateful than I am right now." Jeremiah Edwin Taylor, J.E.T! J.E.D. held and talked to the baby for hours, telling him stories of years gone by. Some were funny, some were serious, some were sad, and all along J.E.D. gave baby J.E.T. words of encouragement.

As the visit came near an end, J.E.D. said, "I've been doing a lot of praying and I have a request with the Lord. As you well know, I have been in a lot of situations that I wouldn't have come out of if it wasn't for the Lord. I've always kept my faith in him and he's always pulled me through."

J.E.D. continued, "I always knew there was a special strength or presence with me, although I never saw it physically. Now I know what it was. An angel of the Lord was with me through everything. He was always there, in every battle, sometimes fighting with me, sometimes fighting for me. The stronger I was in the Lord, the stronger the angel's presence was with me."

J.E.D. looked back to the baby J.E.T. and said to him, "If you follow in my footsteps, you will encounter things I never dreamed of. But don't be afraid because the Lord has granted me two special requests.

"The first is that you will get a warning sign when danger is near. This will be in the form of a jingle from a boot spur, like the ones I wore years ago. My second request is that the Lord give you my guardian angel. I've prayed and fasted about this and knew the Lord would answer this prayer."

J.E.D. knew the Lord had given him one of the special guardians. Because of his dedication to fighting for good over evil, J.E.D. had needed a special angel. At that moment, there appeared before J.E.D. and his family J.E.D.'s guardian. They were all astonished at how huge he was. He appeared to be about six feet six inches tall and had to weigh about 290 pounds, not counting his wings. The angel's muscles looked like they had been poured from molten steel, then forged by the Master Sculptor. When he appeared, it was almost like lightning flashed in the room.

The angel's shoulders were so wide it looked as if he wore cannonballs on each side. If he were a man he would have had to turn sideways to go through doors. His waist didn't look any more than thirty-two inches around, with legs the circumference of tree trunks, and we're not talking post oaks. The angel's wingspan was probably fourteen feet, with the shape of eagle wings. The guardian's head appeared to be shaved. He had dark eyes, high cheekbones, a straight nose, a little gap in his front teeth and a slightly square jaw. He was ruggedly handsome and all warrior. As J.E.D. looked into his guardian's eyes he could see the love of God and his devotion for J.E.D. Although his eyes were almost black as coal, J.E.D. felt a calming sensation, that the guardian would be there for J.E.T. as he'd always been there for him.

As J.E.D. was thanking the Lord for keeping his hand over him and thanking the Lord that he would keep his hand over J.E.T., the guardian raised his eyes toward heaven. He then stretched his hands toward baby J.E.T. as J.E.D. held him. J.E.D. gave the baby to the guardian.

Though the back side of the angel's hands looked like steel, his palms appeared as gentle and caring as J.E.D.'s. With a slight grin, the guardian held and looked at the baby. A few moments had passed when the guardian looked up and nodded his head as if he had been given an order. Then there appeared another angel in their presence. More lightning.

This angel had long, flowing shoulder-length blonde hair and dark blue eyes. He was every bit as big as J.E.T.'s guardian and just as much a warrior. Whether he walked or floated, no one knew. When he stood beside J.E.D. he pulled his wings together behind him. His every muscle seemed taut and ready for action.

The Lord wasn't about to leave J.E.D, this warrior of a man, without protection. J.E.D. took one look at his new angel and knew he was in good hands.

"Fear not, J.E.D.," said his former guardian. "My name is ZAR and I will protect J.E.T. as I have protected you and other great men before you. He will be a warrior, like you have been a true warrior." After the guardian spoke, he gave baby J.E.T. back to J.E.D. and both angels disappeared.

With gratitude in their hearts, J.E.D., Frank and Sabrina began to thank the Lord for this wonderful event and for the protection that had been given to baby J.E.T.

CHAPTER TWO

FRANK AND SABRINA ALSO LIVED in Arizona, but near Flagstaff, so it wasn't feasible for them to go and see Grandpa J.E.D. in Phoenix as often as they would have liked. But during the next couple of months, they went to visit him every other weekend because they could see him getting feebler by the visit.

It was Memorial Day weekend when Frank brought the family for another visit with J.E.D. Frank and Sabrina had another son. His name was Whit and it fit him perfectly. Thirteen months older than J.E.T., Whit already had a great sense of humor. And, at this age he was into everything—he was a handful. He wasn't at J.E.D. and J.E.T.'s first visit because Kenna and Colette were watching him so that J.E.D. could devote all his strength to getting acquainted with J.E.T.

Ding-dong went the doorbell. "I'll get it," Kenna said to J.E.D. As she opened the door, Whit came bouncing in. He hugged Kenna's leg and then went running to J.E.D, babbling the whole time. J.E.D. hugged that little boy, looked him in the eye, and said, "*Osiyo.*"

Automatically, Kenna took J.E.T. from Frank. She hugged Colette and Frank and then went to her rocker. She felt like she was in heaven holding that baby.

A few minutes went by until J.E.D. couldn't stand it anymore. Kenna knew it and wasn't surprised when he asked her if he could hold the baby boy.

With both boys on his lap, J.E.D.'s stories began to flow. Maybe it was because he felt his time was almost gone. Or maybe it was just that he loved talking to Whit and J.E.T. and didn't want to miss an opportunity to lead them to see how wonderful the Lord is.

"I've told you boys many stories about when I was a deputy U.S. Marshal, but now I'm going to tell you about the day that was the best and the worst day of my career. And it was the same day.

"I was on my way to the courthouse in Muskogee to testify in a trial when I stopped to visit a friend. His name was Thunderwolf and he was a Lighthorseman, a mounted police officer for the Creek Indian tribe near Okmulgee.

"It was about 6:00 in the morning when I found Thunderwolf's teepee near the tribal council's building. He was watering and grooming his horse, a big, beautiful, leopard Appaloosa. If you weren't Thunderwolf, you had better not get on that horse. As I approached the teepee, Thunderwolf just looked up and grinned. He probably heard or smelled the big Tovero paint I was riding long before he could see us."

Although he was a man of few words, Thunderwolf had no problem communicating. He preferred Creek, his native tongue, but was fluent in English too because he had lived at the Sequoyah Indian School in Tahlequah until he was about fourteen years old. Thunderwolf and J.E.D. had been in some dangerous situations and had supreme confidence in each other's ability. But J.E.D.'s fondest memory was when Thunderwolf had given his heart to Jesus about four years earlier.

"*Osiyo, chooch!*" J.E.D. teasingly said to Thunderwolf in Cherokee, knowing he preferred Creek over Cherokee. "I have to testify in court this afternoon. Just thought I'd stop by on the way and see how you're doing," he said as he slid off that big paint.

"Going somewhere?" J.E.D. asked, already knowing the answer.

"I've smelled the fire and felt the drums of a forty-nine a few miles away for most of the night," Thunderwolf said, looking to the east. "They've had plenty of time to wrap it up. I guess I'll have to wrap it up for them."

A forty-nine is a drinking party, held away from the rest of the tribe because it's illegal to have alcohol on a reservation. In earlier years it was sometimes a ceremony to prepare for war.

"Do you want to go with me?" asked Thunderwolf as the grin slowly disappeared off his tanned face. Whenever Thunderwolf gave you a chance, whatever the situation was, you had better take it. J.E.D. knew this firsthand.

Without hesitation, J.E.D. said, "Let's do it," as he swung his leg back over the black and white stallion.

Very few words were spoken as the two rode east toward the fork of the North Canadian River. This was preparation time for both of them. Scenarios of what might be in store went through their minds as they expected the worst and hoped for the best. There was no time for shallow prayers to go up that morning. There were no shallow answers and there never are.

J.E.D. had changed from boots to moccasins on the forty-minute ride, something he had learned from Thunderwolf, because there would probably be some reconnaissance to be done when they got to the forty-nine.

When they arrived at the North Canadian River, J.E.D. and Thunderwolf split up briefly to gather intelligence. They knew not to go storming into a forty-nine drinking party, no matter how small or big it was, because the participants could get hostile in a hurry.

J.E.D. and Thunderwolf decided it would be best to cross the Canadian just south of the forty-nine. There were too many briar patches everywhere else and the noise might give away their position.

They left the horses and entered the water. It felt warm compared to the crisp morning air. The outer edges of the forty-nine trickled down to the bank of the river, but most of it was in a clearing just past a line of trees near the bank.

Something seemed a little strange to J.E.D., and then he heard the jingling of spurs even though he wasn't wearing any. The drums had become more intense as they neared the forty-nine. Now, as they came out of the water, the drums slowed. There was almost an eerie feel to them.

As Thunderwolf and J.E.D. approached the first Indians, Thunderwolf said to them, "You've been here all night; you've had your fun. Now pour out your fire water and go home."

They agreed to do it. There was a look in the Indians' eyes that said they were glad Thunderwolf and J.E.D. were there. They didn't express their usual disdain for the white man's law.

As the two walked into what they thought to be the outskirts of the forty-nine, Thunderwolf and J.E.D. realized there were hundreds of Indians and that they were there for Thunderwolf. J.E.D. was just a bonus.

They had never seen a forty-nine this big. This one was actually a ceremony for taking out Thunderwolf, for the Indians felt he was part of the white man's law. They respected him when they were sober, but when they got some fire water in them it was a different story.

As the Indians turned to face Thunderwolf and J.E.D., their drums gave one last beat. They all had pistols, rifles, bows and arrows—you name it—aimed at the two. The hatred in their eyes showed they could hardly wait to end Thunderwolf and J.E.D.'s lives.

The leader, Red Tail, came up to Thunderwolf and said in their native tongue, "What took you so long," as he waved his pistol within inches of Thunderwolf's face.

As J.E.D. looked over the 300 or so Indians, looking for any weakness he could find, he heard Thunderwolf say, without a flinch or even a twitch, "If you want to make it home alive, you better go, NOW!" Even as outnumbered as they were, he knew Thunderwolf meant it.

With only the crackling of the fire breaking the deadly silence, J.E.D. felt a small rumble move the ground beneath his wet moccasins. As he waited either for Red Tail to call everyone off or for Thunderwolf to make this Red Tail's last sunrise, J.E.D. saw a wave of absolute fear come into every one of the Indians' eyes.

Red Tail still had his gun in Thunderwolf's face when he noticed all the other Indians putting down their weapons. As Red Tail's rage increased, J.E.D. watched him fix his eyes on something over Thunderwolf's shoulder. The same fear that had struck the other 300 now struck Red Tail.

J.E.D. turned around to see what had frozen these men in their tracks. He could see only that the fog had rolled in from the river. When he looked back at Red Tail, he saw his grip beginning to loosen on the gun and Red Tail said, in a barely audible voice, "You really are a Lighthorseman." He was so frozen with fear he could hardly turn around to leave.

J.E.D. stood there, astonished at what he had just witnessed. With hundreds of weapons aimed at Thunderwolf and him, he just knew he was standing there in his last pair of wet moccasins. J.E.D. looked Thunderwolf in the eyes and said, "What was that, amazing grace?"

Thunderwolf just grinned his little grin and they turned back to watch the last of the Indians disappear into the trees. Thunderwolf and J.E.D. were thankful deep in their hearts and there were songs of praise on their lips as they headed back to Thunderwolf's teepee.

CHAPTER THREE

WHEN J.E.D. MET THUNDERWOLF AT his teepee, Thunderwolf's Guardian, OLZ, had been anticipating ZAR's return with J.E.D. They had fought many battles together. Every day that ZAR and OLZ got to fight the demonic powers and their puppets, the better that day was.

On the way to the forty-nine, even before J.E.D. and Thunderwolf could crash that party, ZAR and OLZ were crashing and smashing the party of the demons that were with the forty-niners.

ZAR had always enjoyed fighting alongside OLZ. OLZ was also one of the special agents that the Lord sent to protect his protectors. He was dark-skinned, with long black hair that flowed down to his lower back. His dark eyes were always in search of danger that might come Thunderwolf's way. OLZ wasn't quite as tall or as thick as ZAR but you could tell he had the same Master Sculptor.

As they neared the forty-nine, some of the demonic scouts attacked ZAR and OLZ, delaying their arrival alongside J.E.D. and Thunderwolf.

ZAR and OLZ had fought together often and they recognized these scouts to whom they had given beatings many times before. Nasty gashes, marks, even dents remained from those beatings. Now these beasts were looking for revenge.

ZAR had been riding on the big paint's rump when he first saw the demon scouts coming to intercept them. He stepped off that white-face paint stallion. OLZ had been flying. He lit on the ground and pulled his wings in for battle—today it was ground war.

The demon scouts thought they had it made because ZAR and OLZ's swords were still in their sheaths. Silly demons, they never learn.

ZAR's sword was fastened to the left side of his body but he could draw it with either hand. He let the first two demons surround him.

Just as they were about to overtake him, he pushed the handle of his sword backward, catching the demon behind him in the upper thigh. ZAR knew that gouge was going to need some immediate attention.

ZAR then thrust the handle of his sword directly forward out of its sheath. It hit the other demon directly in the chest, putting a dent in it that matched the one ZAR had given it years ago. ZAR was just getting warmed up. As the demons came, he was supplying the heat.

OLZ's sword was in its scabbard, strapped to his back on a slight angle, so that when he drew it with his right hand it always gave a crushing blow.

OLZ liked ZAR's way of setting up the demons—wait 'till you see their bloodshot eyes. Just as one of the demons flew over OLZ, another was attacking to his right. OLZ drew his mighty sword. He gashed the demon above and slashed the demon to his right before the first demon came crashing down. OLZ thought, *There's nothing like a two-for-one special.*

It took ZAR and OLZ about twenty-five minutes to dispense with the waves of demonic scouts that were sent against them. Although that's not a long time, ZAR hated to be away from J.E.D.'s side, even for a second.

With J.E.D.'s God-given skills and intelligence he had been able to handle himself quite well through the years, and ZAR hadn't been late yet.

As ZAR and OLZ crossed the North Canadian, fog enveloped them. The Indians on the bank had joined the others so the two Guardians made their way to the tree line. ZAR and OLZ didn't like what they saw. This was unfortunate for Red Tail and his followers.

ZAR had a way of showing his displeasure when J.E.D. was in danger. He began to growl in such a low tone it would make the ground quake. With a glance upwards, ZAR and OLZ got the signal from the Lord to make themselves visible.

They began to walk out of the fog at the tree line. ZAR's eyes were scanning all the natives with weapons while OLZ's were fixed on Red Tail. As they walked toward Thunderwolf and J.E.D, their eyes pierced everything they looked at. Their physiques glistened like the morning sun and the forty-niners knew they were looking at total destruction.

ZAR and OLZ crossed paths as they got behind J.E.D. and Thunderwolf, with ZAR to J.E.D.'s left and OLZ to Thunderwolf's right. As ZAR and OLZ stopped, Red Tail was frozen with fear looking into OLZ's eyes. ZAR drew his sword with a huge arc and scraped its tip on the ground. When he brought it back to its ready position the tip was as a fireball. Not only did the Indians drop weapons, their jaws dropped and their eyes bugged out.

The standoff was over. The natives knew they were outnumbered and knew if they wanted any chance to live, they had better leave immediately, if not sooner.

CHAPTER FOUR

J.E.T. AND WHIT BARELY MOVED a muscle as they listened to their great-grandpa J.E.D., and neither did Frank or Sabrina. Kenna was in the kitchen making Frank's favorite, blackberry cobbler.

"Keep on," Kenna told J.E.D. Even though she had heard these stories many times, she still enjoyed them all, just not the scars that some had left.

J.E.D. continued as he held the boys tight.

"As Thunderwolf and I were nearing his teepee, I told him I had plenty of time to stop at the Union Indian Agency in Muskogee and tell his boss how good a job he was doing before court that afternoon. Thunderwolf, knowing good and well he wasn't going to talk me out of it, just said, 'Godspeed, my friend.' I turned that Tovero stud east and settled in on the four-hour ride ahead.

"On the ride to Muskogee, all I could think of was how special the Lord is and the many times he had blessed me. I thought, *How did we just get out of that mess without a fight, much less with our lives? There were 300 of them.*

"After I got to the Union Indian Agency, I took the big paint to the livery stable about a block from the courthouse so he could get fresh water and grain and get freshened up a little while I was in court. As I left the stable, there was a wanted poster on the side of the building. It read, 'Dead or Alive, Jack Cinder, $10,000,' and it hadn't been taken down yet. It didn't look like a professional job; it looked like it was maybe five-and-dime quality from Woolworth's.

"I made it to the courtroom about thirty minutes before I was to testify.

"There was an open seat next to Sheriff Gaines, so I sat right down. From the look on his face, I could tell he was happy to see me.

"Sheriff Gaines asked me what had taken so long. 'I thought you would have been here hours ago.'

"I told him, 'I'm right on time. Besides, I had a party to go to this morning. Why, what's up?'

"'I heard that Cinder's gang was coming to town today and I need all the guns I can get. I put a posse together and spread them around town, hoping not to get caught off guard.' As the sheriff was telling me this, I looked over at the defendant's desk and there sat Jack Cinder. His eyes hadn't left me since I walked in the door and even though he had a cold stare, his soul burned with brimstone."

Jack Cinder had started his evil ways many years before, although he was now only in his thirties. It was said he had been born to a loving family and at about the age of nine months he got very sick. He was put in a hospital and quarantined. The doctors wouldn't allow his mother or father to visit him for almost three months. After Jack was released to his family, he was never again the same. He couldn't receive love or give it.

The story goes that Jack's dad was a prominent attorney back east. "Philadelphia, I do believe," said J.E.D. Although his dad tried to give Jack all his love and support, it just wasn't to be.

Jack would bite and hit most any child that came around. He did this to his mother too, and all before he started school. His school happened to be the most prestigious in Philadelphia but, because of his attitude, his teachers were unable to teach him much of anything.

Jack had no interest in school and didn't have any friends, so he filled his time by setting fires in the alleys. Sometimes he would throw a cat into the fire just to hear it scream. It seemed that he had no control over anything but the fire, so this became his only way of feeling adequate in life.

By the time he was ten or eleven, he would steal about anything he could from the stores and, since he wasn't learning anything at school, he rarely went to school.

At fourteen he got drunk one day, robbed a local merchant's store, "rolled" a couple of homeless men and got caught. This took him off the streets for a few years but it didn't do him any good.

Cinder was sent away to an industrial school this time, where he was soon housed with adult prisoners. He may have thought he knew the ways of the world, but now he was being given a crash course in violence, "cell-block style."

Lon Ray was the superintendent of this reformatory and he thought the attainment of "moral purification" was best achieved by fear. So when Jack Cinder misbehaved, even a little, he would get physically abused by the superintendent and then get put in "the hole." Jack was getting lifelong lessons from everyone around him.

"Jack was almost twenty and nearing the end of his sentence at the reform school when two dear Christian ladies went to visit him," J.E.D. continued

"They had a nice visit and Jack told me he felt a tugging in his heart when the ladies talked about Jesus. Although this could have had a happy ending, it didn't. Instead of accepting Jesus that day, he said his 'pride and desires' got in the way and in turn he became meaner and more bitter toward the world.

"When Jack got out, he headed west. He made his way to Wyoming, then went down to Arizona and finally made it to eastern Oklahoma, all the while committing more heinous crimes than he had before. He picked up some no-good rustlers along the way as well. Cinders' countenance had been dark ever since he was released from the hospital but by this time, he was so grim that all he needed was a hood and a cape.

"Cinder and his gang had killed a bank teller at the bank on Broadway Street in Muskogee a few months earlier. He had taken a liking to using a knife and what he did to the teller was going to reward him with the death penalty. But I was going to have to tell the jury he had been doing the same thing in other states, maybe not as heinous but progressively worse. Then I would have to take him to the Territorial Prison in Laramie, Wyoming, on Con-Rail to wrap up some other cases before he was to receive his just dues.

"Judge Little was presiding over the trial. He was always fair and was therefore respected in that part of the country. His name fit him perfectly; he was about five foot three and had a great sense of humor.

"Every time I would see him and say, 'Hi, Judge Little,' he would always tell me, 'I may be small, but I'm Little.' But when he put the robe on, he was all business.

"Sitting there in the courtroom, I had been noticing that Judge Little wasn't looking very well.

"'Sheriff Gaines,' I asked, 'Has the judge been feeling alright lately?'

"Sheriff Gaines said, 'He has been looking a little pekid and moving his left arm and shoulder a lot, kind of like they may be sore, but that's about it.'

"Just then, Judge Little called for a fifteen-minute recess. This wasn't like him. He was usually the marathon man, with no recesses, and he would rarely even have a drink of water. I had noticed him drinking two glasses of water since I arrived.

"Judge Little went to his chambers. Sheriff Gaines and I followed, while Muskogee County's finest stayed with Jack Cinder.

"'Judge Little how are you feeling?' I asked, knowing that he wasn't doing well at all.

"'I feel like I have a wagon wheel on my chest and my arm is going to fall off. This pressure is unbearable!' the judge said, barely above a whisper.

"'Sheriff, is the judge's horse and carriage hooked up alongside the courthouse?' I asked.

"'Sure is,' the Sheriff said.

"'Help me get the judge in the carriage and go get Doc Hill. Take him down to Dwayne T.'s over on Mill Street, I got an idea!' I said, while my brain was turning.

"Dwayne T. supplied all of the dynamite for the rock quarries in the area and I was hoping he was using the same kind as he had for the last few years. He would always order too much and it would get a little crusty sometimes before it would be used. Dwayne T.'s was only about six blocks away but I was praying that wasn't too far for Doc's sake.

"On the way there, Judge Little couldn't help but tease me. 'J.E.D, I hope you make a better doctor than a chauffeur, 'cuz you sure can't drive this buggy worth a hoot. That's not a mule, ya know!'

"'Don't worry Judge, the Lord brought something to my remembrance that a doctor had told me some time ago,' I said, trying to reassure the judge.

"As we arrived at Dwayne T.'s, I could tell that the judge wasn't going to last much longer. 'Dwayne T!' I yelled.

"'Yah!' he hollered back, as he opened the door to his shack.

"'Do you still have some of that old crusty dynamite'? I asked.

"Dwayne T. said, 'Yeah! And whose TNT are you calling crusty,' with a smile, as he recognized who I was.

"'Help me get Judge Little to the dynamite shack,' I said hurriedly.

"'What?' Dwayne T. asked with a puzzled look on his face.

"'No time to explain. Let's get him over there,' I responded.

"Dwayne said, 'You better walk on air in there.'

"We opened the door, gingerly I might add, and I was thinking, *If this doesn't work, nothing will.* Instantly, Dwayne and I got these excruciating headaches while Judge Little immediately started to feel better.

"About then Sheriff Gaines and Doc Hill arrived. 'J.E.D, how's the judge and why did you bring him here?' The Sheriff asked as he tiptoed up to the dynamite shack's door.

"As Doc Hill was checking on Judge Little, I explained to the Sheriff and Dwayne T. why I had brought the judge there.

"Several years before this, I had recovered some stolen nitroglycerin dynamite. It had been sitting in a shack long enough to get a little crusty. While recovering the dynamite, I got a tremendous headache. I mentioned this in passing to a doctor I used to know and he said that the nitro opens up all the blood vessels in your head, which in turn it gives a person a headache.

"So, when Judge Little said he felt all the pressure on his chest, the nitro came to my mind. I thought that since it opens up my sinuses and blood vessels, maybe it's strong enough to open up a Judge's chest.

"'That was good thinking,' Doc Hill said, as he came out of the shack. 'He's getting better by the minute.'

"'The Good Lord deserves all the credit here. If he hadnt brought the story back to my remembrance and answered a few prayers on the way over here, we might have lost the judge,' I said thankfully.

"'You're absolutely right,' Doc Hill said as he started rubbing his head and squinting his eyes, fighting his own headache.

"'Doc, I think the Sheriff and I will go back to the courthouse and check on the deputy and Jack Cinder. Sheriff's a little leery of this defendant,' I said as we helped the judge out of the shack.

"'Dwayne, can I use your horse for a bit while you and Doc take care of the Judge?' I asked as I looked at the bay tied up next to Dwayne T.'s shack.

"'Go ahead J.E.D, we'll be here finishing up on our headaches,' Dwayne said as he tried to keep his eyes in the shade.

"When the sheriff and I got back to the courthouse, he dismissed the jurors until further notice. I looked over at Jack Cinder when the jury was dismissed and for a moment thought I saw a sparkle in his eyes, but on second thought I figured it was probably just a smoldering ember.

"'Hey Marshal, you can't stop it and you can't contain it, you can't even slow it down,' Cinder said to me.

"'Okay, I'll bite, what are you talking about?' I asked

"'Oh, nothing, but you'll soon find out,' Cinder responded and turned his head away."

J.E.D, the sheriff and the deputy got Cinder back to the jail without incident. The sheriff was happy about that and the fact that the judge looked like he was going to be alright but was grumbling nonetheless that there wasn't a verdict yet.

"'Sheriff, since you have this under control, I'm going to see how the judge is doing and I'll keep close tabs on him throughout the night,' I said, knowing that the longer Jack Cinder was in town the better the chance of his gang causing serious problems for Muskogee. As I rode past the bank on 4th Street everything looked normal, but everything felt wrong and nothing felt right.

"I wasn't quite sure of the exact time but I was thinking the bank should have been closed by now, with the shades pulled down. The glare off of the windows made it impossible to see inside so I pulled the bay over to the boardwalk and slid off him. Almost impossible to keep the spurs quiet yet, somehow, they were. I slowly made it up to the glass doors. As I stood at the bank doors, the spurs jingled.

"Still at a disadvantage, I stood outside for a few more moments but it felt like a week. Very little activity that I could tell—no one going in and no one coming out.

"When I opened the door, I saw a teller, Margaret Mayes, where she usually was. But when she saw me, that's the moment that I will never forget.

"The lack of hope and the despair on her face were so great it was gut wrenching, and this only preceded the disaster that the Cinder gang brought. And the earth quaked..."

CHAPTER FIVE

ZAR GLIDED OVER J.E.D. AND his steed on the way to Muskogee, while continually studying the landscape for any signs of danger. There was movement that stayed south of their position almost all the way to Muskogee. Although he knew who it was that was following them, he was more concerned with the spirits that accompanied him.

Those spirits out of a bottle were always wrecking human lives and today there was to be no exception.

Yellowfoot had been at the forty-nine that morning and had tasted his share of the skull and crossbones. His appetite for J.E.D. and Thunderwolf's destruction had been fueled by Red Tail's words but had not been satisfied.

Seeing ZAR and OLZ at the forty-nine, he had been the first to run. But the more he drank, the more the spirits had control over his mind and he couldn't keep from wanting J.E.D. and Thunderwolf dead.

ZAR hovered over the Union Indian Agency. He didn't go inside with J.E.D, knowing the thick stone walls would stop most any weapon around. So he waited outside, keeping an eye on Yellowfoot and his spirit goons.

Yellowfoot worked his way to the north side of the building and climbed a big oak at the top of the ridge, about a hundred yards away. With his single-shot Winchester in tow, he made it about twenty-five feet up, with a few missed foot placings along the way. He figured he had better not go any higher. Nestled in the tree, his anticipation grew with each passing minute.

The goon squad was having quite a time with Yellowfoot. With every missed step their laughter grew louder. They knew he wouldn't last much longer in the tree and would come down one way or another, probably not slowly, probably hard, and sooner rather than later.

The goons had a plan to hit ZAR with everything they had and run but to leave a goon behind to keep Yellowfoot incensed. Nothing they had tried before against ZAR had worked, so why not try this?

When J.E.D. came out of the agency and mounted that big Tovero paint, ZAR had already descended and become a barrier for J.E.D., all the while devising a plan of his own. As J.E.D. took the short switchback trail and headed east down the ridge, ZAR knew that at the second turn J.E.D. would be in a small clearing—a perfect spot for Yellowfoot's single shot. ZAR also thought the goons, too, were going to make their move there.

At the first turn, ZAR had already made his move. He ran along the edge of the ridge before the goons could even twitch. He arrived without a sound. He dismantled the band of goons with blows from his sword and blows from his hands. He sent them back to their destitute land.

There was no time to spare. ZAR looked back at J.E.D., who was almost to the clearing. With a tremendous leap that seemed effortless, ZAR landed none too soon on the branch next to Yellowfoot.

ZAR extended his wing just as Yellowfoot's shaky finger pulled the trigger. Just as the tip of ZAR's wing reached its position, the hammer fell.

Yellowfoot was bewildered and became even more incensed. No kick, no repeat from the Winchester, nothing. Looking over the rifle, wondering why it didn't fire and seeing J.E.D. ride off into the timber, he was ready to scream.

Defying gravity, ZAR leaned over and directed his patented growl into the Indian's ear. It rumbled all the way down to his feet. Total fear came over Yellowfoot. He dropped the rifle, lost his balance and died before he hit the ground. "Fatal distraction, it works every time," ZAR said as he flew away.

What was once a man driven by the spirits of the skull and crossbones would soon just turn into dust and bones.

ZAR returned to his faithful position alongside J.E.D. Looking over the darkened sky of Muskogee, especially the courthouse, he anticipated what dangers lay ahead for him and J.E.D. So far, the day had brought many victories for the Lord. ZAR was eager to bring more and would soon get his chance.

As J.E.D. stepped out of the livery stable, ZAR got into position directly behind him. He floated about three feet off the ground and his wings barely moved.

ZAR's main attention was drawn to the courthouse. He was thinking that the big boys—Lust, Greed, Mayhem—were in town because he had recognized so many of those cronies buzzing around the building and trying to cause confusion.

A couple of cronies had buzzed by ZAR, just for fun. But when they were left on the ground missing a few important body parts, via ZAR, it just wasn't fun anymore.

Once inside the courthouse, it felt like a deep, dark hole. Demonic spirits were in every corner and crevice, save for a few angels that were there to protect the judge, the sheriff and a few others.

There was an extra big boy today. It was the demon Rage. ZAR wasn't too worried about Lust and Greed, but when Mayhem and Rage got together they could stir up trouble in the blink of an eye.

The cronies from the Perjurer demonic realm were attacking the jurors, and trying to confuse them, all day long. ZAR looked at the main crony and said, "You're just a pack of lies."

The crony looked at ZAR and just said, "Well, you're right there." Not really wanting to fight the big Guardian, he just backed off for a little bit and said under his breath, "It's all fun and games until the Guardians show up."

Judge Little and Sheriff Gaines' protectors were keeping their positions, which in turn kept the judge's and the sheriff's minds clear for the task at hand.

ZAR knew his place was at J.E.D.'s side, for the same purpose, and that's where he would remain until the time was right.

Despite all the stares and sometimes a few taunts by the demons, there was still no attack. ZAR figured there would be another time and place for battle, even though it appeared the angels were outnumbered. Even when Judge Little became ill, still no attack.

ZAR and RACE, the judge's protector, escorted J.E.D. and the judge to Dwayne T.'s. With an occasional crony dropping by but not getting up again, there was no real threat.

When they got to the dynamite shack, ZAR gave a mighty blow just as J.E.D. and Dwayne T. stepped inside. That caused them to be walking on air so there was no danger of the old, unstable dynamite blowing up. With this, RACE gave an extra blow for some of the nitro fumes to enter the judge's lungs.

ZAR and BECK, the sheriff's protector, escorted J.E.D. and Sheriff Gaines back to the courthouse so they could help take Jack Cinder to his jail cell. When they got back to the courthouse, all the demons were gone, 'cept for Cinder's.

ZAR knew Rage and Mayhem were up to something and it wasn't too far away. He could see a storm brewing down on Broadway and Main and this time it was more than a twister.

ZAR hovered over J.E.D. as they neared the bank. The sky reminded ZAR of a black hole full of demons, demons going into the bank and none of them coming out. As J.E.D. dismounted the bay, ZAR gave a little blow to the spurs. This helped quiet them just enough for J.E.D. to get near the door with minimal noise.

ZAR floated over to the plate glass window, fully aware that J.E.D. couldn't see inside. ZAR watched as the carnage was about to unfold. He knew it was only him and J.E.D. this time.

ZAR drew his sword with a sweeping arc and its tip scraped the boardwalk, producing a weapon of choice for ZAR, the fireball. He put the fireball in his left hand and, as he stared into the bank, said, "No deposit, no return." ZAR looked over at J.E.D. and caused his spurs to jingle ever so slightly. As J.E.D. opened the door, ZAR gave him a wry little grin and then his growl seemed to begin from his very toes, and the earth quaked …

CHAPTER SIX

"HEY SARGE!"

"What, Del Rio?"

"When is church?" Del Rio asked, as if he didn't know.

"Church! Are you kidding me? It's about time you started going to church. It's also about time we stopped finding all that porn smut in your cell," the sergeant responded.

"I don't need a lecture right now and it isn't smut, it's art," replied Del Rio, as he tried to believe what he had just said.

"Okay, Da Vinci," Sergeant Fred Williams said, with more than a hint of sarcasm. "Church is in fifteen minutes."

Del Rio was perched on the second tier of the cell block. Since he thought he was better than all the other inmates, this is where he stayed most of the time, looking down over them.

Tim Del Rio—Styx was the nickname given to him as a boy—had been so mean as a child that his stepfather told him not only was he named after a river, but he had come from that river in Hell itself.

"Sarge, just for that wisecrack, I'm not going to church," Del Rio responded, trying to make the sergeant feel guilty and still not quite sure who DaVinci was.

"Okay Del Rio, but it's your loss," the sergeant said.

Fred had worked for the Muscogee County Sheriff's Office for about ten years. All five foot six of him was rock hard; he was one deputy who couldn't be intimidated. This probably came from all those fights he'd been in living on the wrong side of Mill Street, when he and J.E.D. were growing up. He knew who the players were and he'd had Del Rio figured out since he arrived. As the sergeant walked away,

24

he knew Styx wanted him to feel guilty about church but he wasn't going to let him.

The sergeant knew that Styx was a player, a small one but a player nonetheless. This was due to his young age but, given time, if Styx had his chance he would become The Player.

Sergeant Williams was a God-fearing man and could sense several evil spirits working in Del Rio—not just Porn, but Anger and Greed and, the way Styx talked, the spirits Alcohol and Alcoholism too. Every chance the sergeant got, he would study Styx from the watchtower.

As usual, it didn't take much to get Styx angry. Just telling him that missing church was his loss made his anger boil. Even though going to church made him uncomfortable, he thought that by attending he could find out the other inmates' weaknesses. But it was always his own weaknesses he found.

While his blood was boiling, he just had to talk to Case Chesney. Before he could even turn to go downstairs to the phone, it was as if his shadow had started first. His demons were stirring the pot.

"Hello!" said the voice that answered the phone.

"Case, where have you been? I've called you several times today. You better start turning your cell phone on!" Styx's language was laced with the vilest profanity you could imagine.

Case and Styx were cousins, with Case about a year younger. But there was no doubt who was the dominant one. Styx had always been the *jefe*.

"Good news Styx, I got the truck," Chesney quickly responded, not wanting to get chewed out by Styx any more than he had to.

"Well, it's about time," Styx said.

"This truck is perfect, it's just like Simon and Simon's, that early '80s Dodge Power Wagon with a huge bumper push guard." Case thought he had to remind Styx what truck they were using.

"It better be perfect, because if it doesn't do the job it's your hide." It didn't matter to Styx whether Case was family or not; he meant it when he said, "It's your hide."

"Oh Styx, don't worry about it," Case said cautiously.

"Have you made your contacts yet?" Styx asked.

"Last night we had beer and pizza. You won't be disappointed. He really is a speed demon," Case said proudly.

"Okay Case, what about Isis?" Styx asked.

"I talked to her last night, too. She'll be on hand before she has a clue what's going on," Case replied.

"That's what I like to hear. Maybe I'll give her a call, too. Make sure the truck is in good working order and make sure it's tagged. Idiots without license plates get caught in Oklahoma. I'll talk to you later and don't forget my blast."

"Okay Styx, I'll have my cell phone on," Case said, trying not to get in trouble again.

Styx's court date with the feds was coming up soon and his mind was churning, going over every inch of his plan to escape.

The way Styx and Case got into this mess wasn't hard. It had just been a matter of time.

Styx was born just outside of Tucson, in Mirana, Arizona. Foster homes, juvenile detention and jail had been his way of life since he could remember. He was almost born in jail but his mother had bonded out just two days before.

He remembered visiting his mom in jail several times when he was a youngster. He also remembered being with her at the hospital after a boyfriend or ex-husband brought the smackdown to her and to Styx. This happened more often than not, that the smackdown was brought on even though Styx didn't even have the guy's last name.

Styx never knew his father, even though he did have his last name. He was long gone before Styx was even born. Even if Styx had known him, the kind of man his mom attracted wouldn't have done him much good anyway.

Styx's mom was named Chloe, but everyone called her C.C. C.C. had a knack for getting into trouble. Like Styx, C.C.'s father wasn't around when she was growing up. So, she taught Styx everything she knew, from the drinking and drug abuse when he was seven to shoplifting and burglaries that started when he was about nine.

When Styx was nine, he was put in his first foster home. The state took him when it took C.C. for four to ten years on the burglary of a business, a Harley shop.

Styx hadn't seen his mother since and at times wondered why he hadn't covered the "C.C." tattoo on the inside of his left forearm that he got when he was ten.

Styx was about five feet ten inches tall, with a muscular build that he didn't have to work for. In a minute he was going to put those muscles to work. With the help of his personal demons, the pot was boiling over. When Styx turned around from talking on the phone, he saw a kid about his own age giving him major *genllo,* the evil eye.

"What are you looking at, because you better get that look off your face," Styx said with his usual profanity.

"You snake me in line for the phone again, it won't be a look you get." Carlos was a Mexican national and he wasn't backing down as he replied in well-spoken English.

"Let's settle this now," Styx said as they headed toward his cell.

Styx usually fought in the shower in most of the jails he had been in, but the showers at the Muskogee County Jail were too small and within view of the tower. Little did the boy know that when Styx started this ruckus his cellmate, Dave, had gone ahead to their cell to ambush the kid.

Carlos may have been able to hold his own had it just been Styx, but with Styx's cellmate blindsiding him it was a different story. Carlos just might have gotten out of there had he been a high-flying Chuck.

Styx and Dave beat Carlos down before he had time to throw a single punch. This was the earliest fight Carlos had been taken out in. It almost seemed as if both Styx and his shadow were in on the beating. Every punch and every kick felt like two punches and two kicks when they came from Styx. Dave's punches felt like a girl's punches—yeah, Cynthia Rothrock's!

When it was over, Styx and Dave went out and leaned against the railing on the second-floor mezzanine, relishing the delight of the misery they had just bestowed upon Carlos.

They weren't too worried about Carlos being in their cell. It would be a little while before an officer made a walkthrough of the pod and maybe by then Carlos would have crawled out. Plus, the only two people Styx really feared were Sergeant Williams and his brother, Reserve Deputy Deano "The Muscle" Williams. He knew that when they came to fight it was no holds barred! He hated it when the sergeant brought out The Muscle.

"When he gets out of our cell, go get the mop and clean up the blood," Styx said with joy in his voice, partly because he was giving an order and partly because of the dirty deed he had just done.

"I've got a phone call to make and it can't wait any longer." As he headed back down the stairs, darkness led the way.

(ring, ring) "Hello!" said a bordello voice softly. "Muscogee County Jail, collect call from Tim Del Rio, will you accept the call?" the operator said.

"Yes," said the voice on the other end of the line.

"Isis, how you doin', Cuz?"...

CHAPTER SEVEN

"CARHOP, TOMORROW'S THE BIG DAY. You up for it?" Case excitedly asked, "'Cause life as you know it is going to change.'"

"Am I up for it? You must be kidding, Case. This is what I've been waiting for. But Styx better be worth it," Carhop wondered out loud.

"Yeah, he's worth it. I can't wait for you to see him in the heat of the moment. It's like there are two him," Case said, with a kind of twisted adoration.

That's the way Case had always been. He'd always worshiped the ground that Styx contaminated. These second cousins couldn't have been any closer, at least not in Case's eyes.

Case was put into a foster home earlier than Styx. From the time he could write, he always wrote to Styx, even though he didn't get any letters back.

You could tell Case and Styx were kinfolk because they had similar features, only Case wasn't quite as big as Styx and didn't have Styx's attitudinal problem. Case had always been the follower, from the time of their first heist, the Pinky Dinky ice cream truck, to the last bank they robbed, when Styx got caught and Case got away. The only reason Styx didn't drop a dime on Case was because he knew Case would help break him out of jail.

"Carhop, what are you going to do with your share of the ill-gotten booty?" Case asked, thinking of something grandiose.

"I'm a Chevy man; always have been. So I've got to buy the top of the line, a ZO6 'Vette! The Viper may beat it on a straightaway, but in overall power and handing the 'Vette's got it beat. Or maybe I'll just steal one and spend my money on something else."

Carhop, whose real name was Varn Tatum, had a great start in life. He was raised in church. He would attend youth camp, vacation Bible school, gleaners and, always, Sunday school. He even gave his heart to the Lord when he was seven years old. His parents and grandparents were believers and most of his kin were, too.

It was obvious that Styx and Case had been "wired up" through the way they were raised, but not Carhop—he had a family who loved and cared for him.

Carhop started riding go-karts at three years old and racing them at five. There were times his dad would even take him to Tennessee to race on the weekends. To Carhop that was the life, racing and being with his dad.

Carhop naturally progressed up the racing circuit. He went from go-karts to midget stock cars, even to some open-wheel cars. Midget dragsters were on the horizon, too. He was also becoming a good mechanic. Wrenching, racing and being with his dad, it couldn't get any better than that.

Then one clear June morning on I-40 in eastern Arkansas, returning home from racing, Varn and his dad were hit head-on by a person stoned out of his head.

Varn was asleep in the back seat of the dual-cab pickup. He sustained minor injuries but his dad took the brunt of the impact and died just a few minutes after the accident. From that point on, Varn's life had been on a downward spiral. No matter how much his mom, grandparents or even his pastor tried to console him, he wouldn't let them. For a while, Varn just went through the motions. School, church and family just became a slow blur. The only thing that mattered now was going fast and he couldn't do that anymore after he lost his dad. The outlet for his pain was right there in front of him, but he wouldn't turn to the comfort that only God could provide. Instead, he found something else to fill the void. That something else was like a black hole that sucked Varn into it.

One day, Varn was hanging out with Georgie, a juvenile miscreant who lived down the block. Georgie was always calculating something, but Varn never saw it because he hadn't been raised in that type of environment.

"Varn."

"Yeah, Georgie."

"You know, you're a pretty good mechanic," said Georgie, reeling Varn in for his plan. "As good as you are, I bet that I can hotwire a car faster than you can!"

This caught Varn off guard. Varn knew he was a good mechanic but he had never before even attempted to hotwire a car. The whole time he thought, *I can't let Georgie get the best of me. I'm a better mechanic than he is.*

All the while Georgie was thinking, *He's going to fall for this and we'll be joyriding before the hour's up.*

All Georgie cared about or knew was that Varn could wrench and drive, even though he was only fourteen years old. The only thing Georgie could do was hotwire a car. He couldn't wrench or drive because every time he drove, it seemed that he ended up in a ditch and in juvenile hall.

With the dare instituted, the search for the ride commenced. Even though Varn was feeling queasy about this, he was also getting excited.

He said, "Georgie, let's get the tools and go. I've got a date with a rat."

Georgie wasn't quite sure what Varn was talking about, but he was ready to go and get into some trouble. Only this time his trouble had company.

A few blocks from where Varn and Georgie lived was a manufacturing company. Varn seemed to think they used to make winches, but that had been a long time ago and they had changed companies several times since.

Much to Georgie's surprise, there was a plethora of good cars in the lot to "ride."

"Okay Varn, take your pick," Georgie said with delight.

"Take my pick! I knew which one I wanted before we ever got here. Now you find your ride Georgie," Varn said, as he headed toward an early-nineties black Chevy pickup.

Georgie made his way to a mid-nineties Toyota two-wheel-drive 4Runner.

Knowing he could wire the Toyota much quicker than Varn, Georgie feigned difficulty even trying to get the door open. This was Georgie's plan all along. He was never going to try to steal any car; he was going to always let Varn steal it.

As Varn achieved his goal of getting the truck open and started, he called to Georgie. "Hey Georgie, let's go," he said, half pleased as a half-empty feeling came over him.

Georgie couldn't have been happier—he had reeled Varn in, hook, line and sinker. Yes, misery does love company.

"Okay where to now, Carhop?" Georgie asked with glee as they headed north on Garnett Road.

"I've been wanting to drive one of these 454 SS's. I knew they had the power to pull the Titanic, but I didn't think it would be able to pull the USS Batfish behind the Titanic too," said Carhop as he lit up the back tires.

"I have a buddy over in Owosso. Let's hop on over to highway 169 and see how this 454 rat SS breathes," Carhop said as he tried to control the truck in a fishtail.

"By the way, how did you know about this car lot?" Georgie asked.

"My mom works there," Varn responded.

With this "ride" under his belt and since he hadn't got caught, each ride after this would be that much easier, with a little less guilt.

For a moment, Varn thought of the plans he'd had with his dad. He could have been racing at Hallett Raceway, Laguna Seca and more, but now he was in a stolen truck. How plans change. And he was still angry at God.

CHAPTER EIGHT

"THANKS FOR THE RIDE, BRO'," said J.E.T. as he and Whit pulled into Sky Harbor Airport.

"No problem, dude. When did you say you were coming back from Oklahoma?" asked Whit.

"I'll be flying a prisoner back for court on Thursday, so I'll be in Three Wells in about a week," J.E.T. said over the harsh slope of the solid lifter cam in Whit's '69 Camaro Z28 Rally Sport.

"Good. Come by when you get back; I'll have something to show you," Whit said with a mischievous smile.

J.E.T. didn't have time to delve into the mystery. "Okay Bro', I'll see you then. I don't want to keep the cons waiting," J.E.T. said as he turned toward Sky Harbor with a wave goodbye...

J.E.T. was pushing forty now, although he looked like he was in his early thirties. His hair was still black and, along with his high cheekbones, showed some of his Cherokee and Choctaw heritage. There was that chevron mustache with a four-day beard, but the blue eyes were all Irish. At six feet one inch and 215 pounds, he looked like he could play center field for the Yankees. If he hadn't wanted to pursue a law enforcement career, especially with the United States Marshals Service, he probably would have been a major leaguer.

After more than fifteen years with a U.S.M.S. star on his chest, he wouldn't have it any other way. With the rich history of the Marshals Service dating back to President George Washington, protecting and serving his country never sounded corny to J.E.T.

Not long after touchdown, the Amigos skies became ominous. As J.E.T. was getting his rental car at Tulsa International, he thought,

That's eastern Oklahoma for you. It will probably pour down rain before I get to Muskogee.

J.E.T. was wanting to see his oldest and dearest friend, Zane, but this trip was too short so it would have to be just a phone call. Driving the back roads to the Muskogee County Jail from Tulsa led J.E.T. to reminisce. *It's going to rain anyway,* he thought as he turned onto the Coweta exit.

A few things had changed in the more than twenty years since Zane, his cousin Artemis and J.E.T. had burned up those roads. But the still familiar sights and smells were there, like Robert's BBQ, Post Oaks and eastern Oklahoma's rolling hills.

Just east of Coweta, on highway 51B, the rain was coming down hard as he passed over that no-name swollen creek. At first he could barely see it, but he could tell that a car was stopped and partially off of the road. The car's lights were on, but no flashers. J.E.T. pulled up behind the car and turned his flashers on. He knew he was going to get soaked even though he had an emergency rain poncho the rental car had provided.

It's probably nothing, J.E.T. was thinking, but he still had to check it out.

As he got out of the car, J.E.T. heard a little bit of thunder but hadn't seen any lightning yet, maybe because of the tall, thick trees. The stopped car's window was rolled down just enough that he could see a woman inside with a little girl about five years old.

"Lady, what seems to be the trouble?" J.E.T. asked, as drops of rain bounced off of the car's roof and hit him in the eyes.

"I ran through a puddle of water and then my car stalled," the woman said, with uncertainty in her voice.

Just then, J.E.T. heard a familiar but rare "ching ching." *Why here and why now?* J.E.T. thought, as he quickly looked to his right. An even quicker look to his left revealed the push bar of a pickup truck coming right at him. Without the truck's lights on, and with it being so dark because of the storm, it had been impossible for J.E.T. to know the truck was coming at him.

With nowhere to run, J.E.T. did his best Spencer Tillman imitation against Texas. With some vertical leap still in him, he jumped up onto the top of the car and slid down the other side just as the pickup took off the driver-side mirror, and maybe a little extra, as it sped by.

J.E.T. sloshed out of the bar ditch and asked the lady if she and the girl were okay. Using her phone, he got in touch with Coweta's Towing Service to come and give them some help or get them back to town.

Since he only saw the truck for a millisecond, the only features he could remember were the push guard and that maybe it was a Ford. If he didn't have to get to Muskogee to change clothes before going to the jail, he would have contacted Coweta's finest and pursued the incident further.

The warning kept going through J.E.T.'s mind: *Never too late, but it was never too early, either.* Then, as he headed toward Muskogee, his mind drifted back to the first time he'd heard it...

CHAPTER NINE

ZAR DIDN'T USUALLY RIDE SHOTGUN on the inside of a car; he preferred standing on the trunk where he was more accessible.

Today was no different. Since Earth's atmosphere has no effect on ZAR, today's storm had no bearing on him either.

As J.E.T. and ZAR headed toward Muskogee there were a few little flareups of demons along the way, but nothing unusual until J.E.T. stopped to help the lady and her daughter. ZAR could see something brewing and it was quickly headed their way.

ZAR could tell this was no ordinary sinner coming toward them. The size of the entourage was a few hundred more demons than usual. With this kind of following, the demons' numbers only grow more and more with each passing day. With drugs and alcohol, they grow even more.

ZAR walked through the rental car J.E.T. was driving as he started to get resistance. ZAR started encountering the pesky little demon scouts shortly before their host got there. The scouts were discarded like an RC Cola bottle hitting a road sign. Why did they even try, because they'd never succeeded against him?

After ZAR's warmup, he looked around for any lingering demons because he knew he was going to have to leave J.E.T.'s side, hopefully for only a few moments. With the area clear now, ZAR grabbed a pudgy little demon and shot out of there quicker than the demons were expecting, even with the little pudgy one in tow. All the while he thought, *This day is getting better by the minute, fighting for the Lord.*

ZAR needed to get this fight over with fast because the truck was quickly approaching J.E.T. and he needed to be there. As the demons came at ZAR in the shape of an arrowhead, he thought, *They make this just too easy.* With the demon scout by the nape of the neck, ZAR said with some abrasiveness, "To paraphrase humans, here's bowling for demons."

With a throw like that, ZAR would have looked comfortable on the PBA tour. It actually looked a lot like Big Zane's form. The little demon almost curved off of the road but came right back to the center of the highway, so fast that the demons escorting the truck couldn't get out of their own way in time, much less out of the scout demon's path.

That scout demon took out every last one of the escorting demons and none of them were able to get up until J.E.T. was long gone.

ZAR had barely made it back to J.E.T. in time to give him the jingle and help catapult him over the car.

CHAPTER TEN

IT WAS ABOUT EIGHTEEN YEARS ago and he had graduated from the Indian Police Academy a couple of weeks earlier. At the end of his shift, J.E.T. had just served some papers in a little town on the reservation's boundary.

On his way out of town, J.E.T. saw a woman holding a toddler and walking, across the street, about a block away. What looked peculiar was that it was early January and neither of them were wearing coats.

As J.E.T. approached the pair, the woman saw him and frantically walked toward his patrol car. Now J.E.T. knew this wasn't tribal land, so this woman and the toddler were not part of his jurisdiction. But nonetheless, judging by the woman's face, there was a problem.

J.E.T. rolled down his window and before he could ask what they needed, he heard, for the first time, "ching-ching." He thought, *How strange.* His patrol car had been serviced recently and was running fine, so what kind of noise was that?

Within seconds of the "ching," the woman started pleading with J.E.T. "My ex-husband's in there," she said, pointing to the house across the street. "He's violating a restraining order. I have two boys in there and he won't let them out. And officer, he has a gun."

"Okay ma'am, get in the car." The woman and her toddler got into patrol car. To get them warm, J.E.T. gave them a coat and a sweatshirt he had. He then drove them down the block to keep them safe. As he did this, he radioed the town's finest to meet him at his location.

When Officer Nolan arrived, J.E.T. informed him of the situation. Officer Nolan attempted to go up to the house but the ex wouldn't let him get very close.

As officers from the town and Officer Kandigo from the Cheyenne & Arapaho Tribes arrived, they were informed of the situation as well.

Officer Kandigo and the other officers went to the front of the house to try to talk the ex out. Officer Nolan and J.E.T. started trying to find a way into the house, either through a door or a window. As they looked through the living room window, they could see the ex waving around a gun. The two boys were in the room with him.

J.E.T. knew that if they didn't find a way in soon, something bad was going to happen.

It took J.E.T. and Officer Nolan about two minutes to get around the house and find that the side door was unlocked. While Officer Kandigo kept the ex occupied, Officer Nolan entered the kitchen through the side door.

J.E.T. kept thinking that if he could get within seven or eight feet of the ex, he could take him with or without a gun.

Officer Nolan had positioned himself to the left side of the kitchen by one of the two iceboxes. Just as J.E.T. stepped into the house, one of the little boys stepped into the kitchen doorway and saw him. The boy backed out of the doorway and told his dad what he had seen.

J.E.T. quietly stepped back out and pulled the door shut, hoping that the ex, if he looked into the kitchen, would see that no one was there. But instead of just looking into the kitchen, the ex headed straight for the door J.E.T. was hiding behind.

Halfway into the kitchen, Officer Nolan yelled, "Freeze!" With a startle, the ex turned his head toward Officer Nolan. J.E.T. saw his opportunity. The ex was seven or eight feet from the door when J.E.T. busted through it, jumped over a kitchen chair, grabbed the ex's arms, drove him back across the kitchen and crushed him into the other icebox. This happened so fast the ex didn't even have time to turn his head to see what had hit him. J.E.T. was able to take the ex's gun without ever pulling his own. The great physical condition he tried to stay in and the knowledge gained from Indian Police Academy had made this possible. But the confidence came from his relationship with the Lord.

When it was all over and the ex was in Officer Nolan's patrol car, the oldest boy, who was probably eight years old, came over to J.E.T. and said, "Thank you, thank you, sir." That's when J.E.T. knew that being a cop was worth it all.

CHAPTER ELEVEN

ALTHOUGH IT DIDN'T SEEM LIKE it, ZAR had now been with
J.E.T. for twenty-two years. There had not been too many grand
skirmishes with the demonic world, but ZAR knew that now J.E.T.
was out of the police academy, things would be heating up real fast. He
couldn't see the future but with his keen hearing, sharp eyes and the
Lord's insight, he didn't need anything else. When trouble came, he
greeted it before it got there.

Things were starting to stir around the reservation just before J.E.T.
was to get off duty. Before he had pulled out of the driveway, ZAR was
anticipating the action a few blocks down the road.

ZAR had already seen the woman and the child leave the house
and now his eyes were fixated on her ex-husband. He could see the
over-under .38 derringer he was waving around, pointing it at his ex-
wife and children.

With J.E.T.'s intellect, desire and heritage, ZAR knew he was ready
to get his feet wet.

The demons were so thick going into the house that it looked like
black smoke coming out of the chimney, but in reverse.

The demon characters had been a little preoccupied with the
husband before they noticed that ZAR and J.E.T. were right in their
wheelhouse.

As ZAR had seen so many times before, alcohol was the cause of
this mess. *What happened to "live sober?"* ZAR thought, as he was getting
into the middle of all this.

There were no demon sentries, so it was quite a surprise to this evil
axis when ZAR and J.E.T. were right there on top of them.

By the time J.E.T. had stopped and talked to the woman, the demonic cesspool finally noticed that ZAR, their holy arch nemesis, was there, taking every one of them out. One by one, five by five or even fifty by fifty, it didn't matter—they were getting taken out.

What had once been a time full of glee for the demonic scoundrels was now the Hall of Famer against the bush league.

Had they been ready, with their sheer numbers they might have put ZAR and J.E.T. against the ropes. But now, with all the blows ZAR was dishing out, the demons felt like they were getting Rocket Roger's fastballs in the ribs. They would be nursing those wounds on the bench for a while and there would be no ice for their wounds.

While J.E.T. and the Officer Nolan searched the house for any possible entry, ZAR was in full force. With every blow from ZAR, damage was done to those ghouls. While once demons poured into this angry, drunken man, they now flew out of him to get into the middle of the battle with ZAR.

ZAR kept J.E.T. and Officer Nolan between him and the demons while they were finding their entry into the house. ZAR was able to keep the kitchen door quiet while Officer Nolan went through it. But he was so busy fighting when J.E.T. went through it he wasn't able to calm the squeak the door made. Too late, this bitter, angry man heard the squeak and became even more enraged.

Just then, with what must have been a surge in prayer, ZAR's speed, strength and senses became so great that he drove the demons away with every blow. The flow of demons coming out of this angst-ridden man had now stopped. They didn't want any part of the carnage ZAR was giving their mates. They were so scared they quit peeking out of the man, even with their sheer numbers.

At this exact second, ZAR saw that J.E.T. was coming through the door. He knew that J.E.T. wouldn't let Officer Nolan be in the house by himself.

After the job that ZAR had just done on the demons, the only obstacles in J.E.T.'s way were the door and the chair. With J.E.T.'s Bullet Bob quickness, the door and the chair were no obstacle at all. A sly grin came across ZAR's face when he saw J.E.T. take out Mr. Angry without even drawing his weapon, or without the man being able to point his gun at J.E.T.

CHAPTER TWELVE

"WHEN ARE Y'ALL GOING TO get this system up and running again? It's been down for days now," Fred asked with angst in his voice as he talked to Intelex.

"We've been working on it. Our software is just not responding at this time," the voice said with some hesitancy.

"There's word coming out of the pods that something bad is going to happen soon and I need all of my tools to find this silver bullet. When you fix it, call me then and not a minute after," Sergeant Williams said just before hanging up the phone.

Fred knew something was going on and had a sneaky suspicion it was Del Rio as he made his way to the cell tower. "Del Rio is on the phone again, I sure wished Intelex was working so I could hear the calls he's been making," Fred said, not really talking to anyone but just thinking out loud.

"Case, you ready?" Styx demanded more than asked.

"I'm ready, Simon and Simon is ready, Speed Demon's ready, the pliers are ready, and some blast. Yeah, we're ready!" Case replied, with some anxiety in his voice.

"Okay. I've got court in an hour. I need to make one more call," Styx said as he hung up the phone.

(ring, ring) "Isis, how are you doing honey. You haven't had your cell phone on for a few days, have you?" Styx asked, trying not to be mean with cousin Isis.

"Tim, my battery went bad on my cell so I had to get a new one. Sorry, Tim," Isis said.

"Listen to me, Isis, this is very important. I will see you in a couple of days. Have all of the information ready when I see you. You know how that copper company screwed our families out of that land and how much money they've made since then," he proclaimed in a stern voice.

"Okay Tim, I will have all of the information you need when I see you." Isis hung up the phone. She still felt naïve, wondering if Tim was actually telling her the truth. But, sure he would; they were cousins.

Styx was thinking this was the biggest day of his life and that everything had better go right.

"Del Rio, let's go. You have court at eleven!" the deputy yelled from across the pod.

"Ol' right! Ol' right!" Styx yelled back, stalling to give Case a little more time to get into position. "I'll be right there. I have to change my shoes," Styx said, thinking, *Just a few more minutes.*

The deputy put the hard restraints on Styx and led him to the sally port. There, he loaded Styx and about five other inmates into the transport van. With the federal courthouse only about two blocks away, the deputy had plenty of time to get the inmates there.

Pulling out of the sally port onto South 3rd Street, the deputy didn't notice anything unusual. But then, before he could do anything about it, he saw the big push guard on a four-wheel drive pickup about to ram into the driver-side door.

On impact, the deputy's left arm was pinned between the door and the steering wheel. Even worse, he was left-handed. With his arm pinned he couldn't reach for his gun.

Case had been parked down the block at a spot where he had plenty of time to see the courts van exit the sally port. With the torque of the 440 Magnum under the hood of the Dodge Power Wagon, it didn't take Case long to plow into the side of the van.

Case jumped out of the pickup with a big set of bolt cutters. He went to the passenger side of the van and broke out the window. He unlocked the doors and said, "Sorry, Bud." Case grabbed the mic, ripped it out of the dash and took deputy's radio before he slid open the side door.

With the big pair of bolt cutters Case had, he was able to cut the leg irons and handcuffs off of Styx faster than if he would have had to unlock them. He'd just unlock them later. Styx was a little dazed from the crash so Case pulled him out and led him to the passenger side of the pickup. Case turned the pickup around, without a look back, not worried about the deputy who had hit his head on the window and appeared to be knocked out.

Case and Styx headed down Cincinnati Street and turned under the overpass on Main Street. That's where they met up with Carhop.

They jumped out of the Power Wagon and into a similar-looking white Ford pickup. It also had a big push guard. They headed south on Main Street and turned east on Peak Boulevard, from where they took the back roads out of town. "Don't tell me we're taking this to Arizona?" Styx asked, still groggy from the escape.

"No, are you kidding? When we get to Coweta that's when we get our real ride. This is for any roadblocks we might encounter between here and there," Carhop explained happily.

"Don't worry Styx, I told you it's all figured out. Oh, by the way, this is Carhop," Case said, trying to ease Styx's throbbing head.

"Well, no kidding," Styx said, already annoyed at Case.

Styx's demon posse were giddy as schoolgirls. They almost felt like they had been freed from jail themselves. Although they had been causing Styx to stir up trouble while in jail, they knew they could really wreak some havoc on the outs.

As the truck went down the road, it appeared that its shadow was growing and growing. As the weather started to turn for the worse and it got darker, even at mid-morning, the demons felt their prince was going to be there with them.

Little did they remember, but behind every dark cloud there's a double-edged sword.

As the band of demons were getting closer to Coweta, they picked up cast-outs along the way. The more they picked up, the braver they got.

With the rain pouring down, and almost to Coweta, they just knew the plan was going as scheduled.

Along the way, the scouts had been going out and coming back with what intel that they could find. All of a sudden, the prideful demon realized the scouts weren't returning as regularly as they had been during the trip.

But alas, it was too late. Here came one of the midget posse imps all rolled up in a ball and there was ZAR with his best Dick Weber follow-through.

With no time to react, the demons were scattered all over and throughout the post oaks. It must have taken them ten minutes to regroup and catch up with Styx. In that melee, Pride got hurt and wouldn't be forgetting ZAR anytime soon.

As Styx, Case and Carhop approached that no-name swollen creek bridge, Carhop felt the truck jerk into the oncoming lane. With no time to swerve back, he was headed for what appeared to be a stalled car halfway off the road.

"Oh, no!" Carhop yelled as he tried to jerk the steering wheel back to the right to get the truck back on the correct side of the road.

"I'm going to hit him!" Carhop desperately yelled, trying not to hit J.E.T. "Come on, hit him. You can do it," Styx said, coaxing Carhop the whole time.

On a slick road, the truck wasn't responding like the cars Carhop had been taught to drive in. Just as the pickup's brush guard took out the car's driver-side mirror and was about to take out J.E.T., he bounded over the car, and not a millisecond too soon.

Carhop couldn't believe his eyes. "Did you see that? Did you see that?" Carhop asked excitedly.

"Yeah, I did. Some driver you are. You should've hit him," Styx replied with disdain. "If you want to make it to Arizona and back, you had better do what I say, starting NOW!"

Carhop knew he had better watch his p's and q's with this one, or Styx was right—*I won't be coming back.*

CHAPTER THIRTEEN

J.E.T. HAD JUST GOT CLEANED up at the hotel. He went over to the Muskogee County Jail to see about the prisoner he was going to take back to Arizona the next morning.

They all seemed to like J.E.T. down at the county. He always seemed to bring some of that Arizona warmth with him.

Since he had an afternoon to kill, he looked up his cousin Fred.

"*Osiyo.* Would one of you ladies tell the sergeant that I'm here?" J.E.T. asked.

"Sure will, but he's not too happy right now," the admin lady exclaimed.

"Why, what's the problem?" J.E.T. asked. "I think I'll let the sergeant explain it to you," she replied as she called Fred's office.

"Marshal J.E.T., go right on into his office," she said as she pointed toward the sergeant's door.

"J.E.T., we're on lockdown and probably will be for a day or two," Sergeant Williams said, rather angrily. "The reason why we're on lockdown is because your prisoner escaped and put one of our deputies in the hospital."

"Was it Del Rio?" J.E.T. asked.

"Yes, we know someone used a pickup with a big push guard on it and rammed our transport van that was taking him to the federal courthouse for sentencing this morning," Fred said as he tried to remain calm.

"How is your deputy doing, Fred?" J.E.T. asked concernedly.

"Well, he has a slight concussion. It knocked him out for a bit. He also has a broken arm. The X-rays showed some ligament damage so he'll be on light duty for probably half a year," Sergeant Williams said as he was getting more worked up by the minute.

"Sergeant, I almost got run over by a pickup with a brush guard this morning just outside of Coweta," J.E.T. said as he remembered his leap of faith over the disabled car in the pouring rain. "Contact Wagner County Sheriff's Office and Tulsa County Sheriff's Office and find out if they've had any incidents lately with trucks fitting that description."

(ring, ring) "Sergeant, this is Brad from Intelex."

"This better be good news," Fred ordered.

"It is. Intelex is up and running. We found our glitch in the system and fixed it but the best part is the system was still recording. For the last seven days, it's been recording," Brad said, half proud and half embarrassed over the Intelex communication system breaking down.

"We'll talk later. I have some important calls to tend to," Sergeant Williams said as he hung up the phone.

"Sergeant, I'll be back soon. I'm going to run over to the marshal's office and get another cellphone 'cause mine's shot from this morning. It quit working shortly after I saw that truck. I'll see if the area marshals have got any more information on Del Rio and who might be helping him," J.E.T. said as he was already halfway out the door.

"Call me when you get there," Fred said, almost yelling so J.E.T. could hear him through the shutting door.

As J.E.T. walked into the marshal's office, the marshal on duty handed him the phone.

"Deputy Marshal Taylor, it's Fred. We have some good info on Del Rio and we think we know who might be helping him," Sergeant Williams said with a little more excitement in his voice than a few minutes earlier.

"Okay Sergeant, let me see what's going on over here with this and then I'll come back over."

"Sergeant Williams, what have we got?" J.E.T. asked when he returned to the sheriff's office.

"We went back seven days and Del Rio had numerous calls to Case Chesney. We believe him to be Del Rio's cousin and we've totally suspected him in Del Rio's bank robbery conviction," Sergeant Williams said.

"His name is Chesney?" J.E.T. asked. "I remember hearing something about Chesney. Where does he live?"

"This greaser's address is 71st and Garnett, east side of Tulsa," the sergeant said.

"Send Tulsa County's finest to that address and see if the boys were going there," J.E.T. ordered as he put on the headset and started listening to the past week's telephone recordings of Tim Del Rio.

"Sergeant, do you know anything about this Isis that Del Rio has been calling? She's from my neck of the woods," J.E.T. asked.

"It appears that Isis is his cousin as well. I've run a forty-eight and a forty-nine on her, but NCIC comes back clear, no wants or warrants anywhere or at any time. She's never been in trouble," the sergeant said with some wonderment, "and I don't show an address for her, just that she's from Arizona."

"At least not yet," J.E.T. responded. "But I've got a suspicion that Del Rio will pull her down to his flaming depths."

"J.E.T.! Isis got a phone call today from none other than what we believe to be Case's cell phone," Sergeant Williams said with glee. "It pinged near his last address."

CHAPTER FOURTEEN

STYX, CHESNEY AND CARHOP HAD made their way through south Tulsa and on over to the old Route 66. At this time their plan was to get on and off 66 and the other major throughways until they made it to Arizona. But first they had to make it out of Oklahoma.

As the trio were pulling into Sapulpa, Styx informed Chesney and Carhop, with little emotion, "We need to get rid of this truck and get into a car. Start looking, Carhop."

"There's a lake just south of town, I'll drop off y'all at the podunk used car lot. Carhop, get a Buerick; it will be a little less conspicuous. Chesney, distract the owner and don't screw this up. Be at the lake in twenty minutes," Styx demanded.

At the car lot, Chesney started toward the office while Carhop began looking at the inventory.

"Carhop!" "Yeah," Carhop answered, a little preoccupied.

"Do your magic, Carhop. The owner is going to be gone the rest of the afternoon. He left a note on the door that says he's at a funeral," Chesney said giddily.

"Alright, here it is, the 'Buerick', like Styx would say, and it's a Regal GS, Supercharged. I'll be in this car in just aaaa, sseeecccoondd. Just like that. Chesney, did you take notes?" Carhop said proudly of his technique for breaking into cars. "Let's go find the lake and Styx."

With the truck in the lake and the truck tags on the car they were on their way again. "We'll trade these tags later," Styx said. They made it through to Edmond, on to Northwest Highway in OKC, then south through Concho, then to El Reno and on to I-40.

"Going through Concho gave me an idea. When we get to Clinton I'm going to get some money," Styx said restlessly.

As they neared Clinton, Styx saw the sign he was hoping for: "C & A Smoke Shop this exit."

"Carhop, take this exit. When you get to the smoke shop pull in there. We're going to get some spending money," Styx demanded.

Somehow, in Styx's mind, when he demanded something, he thought he was getting respect. He didn't know how to earn respect since he'd earned anything but misery his whole life.

"Chesney, Carhop, see that hospital up the hill? If you don't do exactly as I say, y'all will find yourselves in their ER and you probably won't come out alive," Styx said, using his best threatening voice.

"Carhop, back up on the west side of the trailer. I don't want you to go in, just keep the car running. 'Cause when we come out, it will be time for you to show me what Chesney thinks you have," Styx said, all the while never taking his eyes off the smoke shop. "And if someone drives up and is going to come into the smoke shop, let me know by giving two short blasts on the horn."

Carhop and Case were becoming real uncomfortable about now. They knew this was going to be a warmup for Arizona, but was it just pregame or was it the first pitch?

Beads of sweat started to pop out on Carhop and Case's foreheads, even though it was mid- December.

Styx noticed there was only one car in front of the smoke shop. He thought it was an employee's, not a customer's, which would make this robbery even better.

As Styx and Chesney walked up the wooden steps to the smoke shop trailer, they noticed that the sliding glass door was darkly tinted. What was waiting for them on the other side?

A warm wall of air hit Styx and Case when the door slid open. Initially they saw a black-haired Cheyenne woman who appeared to be in her mid-twenties. Styx thought this would be so easy that he almost smiled. But as they neared the counter, Styx's countenance changed in a hurry.

There behind the counter someone was watching TV. As Styx and Case got almost to the counter, he stood up.

As the man stood, Styx noticed a dark gray uniform and was thinking, *That stinking smoke shop security*. But when he stood all the way up, it was the six feet three inches and thick dark frame that took Styx one step back mentally.

Case hadn't forgotten that when there was more than one person during a robbery, he was to split off from Styx. They thought that by doing this, the victims would keep their eyes on Styx and not Chesney, since Styx was the more aggressive looking one.

"Marlboro, in the red box," Styx half asked, half demanded of the woman, all the while trying not to look at Mr. Security Officer.

With Styx distracting the two employees, Case pulled an easily concealed .38 Special from under his Levi's jacket.

"Big Boy, don't move!" Chesney demanded excitedly as he moved towards the big Cheyenne and Arapaho guard.

Dumb move for Chesney. This Indi'n was big, but he wasn't dumb. Raised on the rez and part of the Pure Indian gang in his younger years, he had seen and been part of enough violence to last many lifetimes. Plus, he had warrior blood running through him from many generations back.

Security guard Danny White Buffalo—once no man put the fear in him; now he feared no man.

He had found the Lord in his late teens and left that gang nonsense behind. He really didn't care for working security at the smoke shop and at the bingo hall but jobs were hard to find on the reservation.

When Case put the .38 in Danny's face, Danny took the gun and part of Chesney's thumb with it. As cat-quick as Danny was, so was Styx. He shot the security guard through the arm with a bullet that lodged in his thick chest muscle.

"Pick up your gun!" Styx told Case in disgust. "Big Boy's gone. Lady, open the cash register... now get to the back of the trailer," Styx ordered, while he nicked the big Indian's cheek with his knife.

Chesney picked up his gun and pulled the phone line out from the wall. As Styx and Chesney left the smoke shop, Chesney pulled out his blade and slashed one of the tires on the car parked outside. He thought if he had slashed two tires it would have brought too much attention, and they would need all the time they could get to get away from there.

"Okay Carhop, get us out of here," Styx said sternly while thinking about how good it had felt when he shot the smoke shop guard.

"Stop at Del Rancho. I'm hungry. 'Cause this is probably the last time we'll ever have their steak sandwiches." For Carhop, that somehow sounded ominous.

Styx had the money counted by the time they got through Clinton. "When we get to Amarillo, get back on Route 66 for a ways, then on and off I-40 and 66 through New Mexico. Destination Phoenix, but ultimate destination, boys, is Three Wells!"

"We have plenty of money 'till then," Styx exclaimed after he ate. He put his head back in his seat and shut his eyes. "Get us another car when we get to Groom!!" Styx demanded.

Carhop felt an eerie feeling come over him when they left Clinton. He felt like he was in a stranglehold with nowhere to go but down.

CHAPTER FIFTEEN

THIS MUSKETEER-LOOKING ANGEL KNEW HE was going to have his hands full by the long black train that was headed toward the smoke shop. As he kept close to Danny, he could sense that a battle was inevitable.

Usually, this angel with long curly brown hair didn't worry about the smoke-shop guard 'cause he always shone when trouble came his way. But today the good Lord hadn't given him the confirmation that everything was going to be alright.

The fight started several minutes before Styx and company got there. The scout demons and imps had heard Styx say where he was going, so they were able to get there first.

BEAME, White Buffalo's guardian, was eager for a battle but it had been a long time since he had seen a train this long. He knew its engineer was becoming pure evil.

It didn't take long for BEAME to dispel the imps and scouts. It was the soldiers and drones that gave him his best fight. There was going to be no room for error on this one.

These demons always try to lure the guardian away from his assignment and this time was no different. But this time, more than ever, BEAME knew he couldn't leave Danny's side, not knowing the outcome.

BEAME preferred the double-double. Two double-edged swords made him almost impenetrable and as he used them the demons became disheartened and confused by the sheer skill that was displayed on them.

The intruders were falling by the numbers as Styx and Chesney walked through the door. The angel knew this probably wouldn't last long but he couldn't afford to become distracted. When White Buffalo stood up to confront Styx and Case, the guardian was there with him. No sooner had Case pulled a gun on Danny than another wave of nasties came his way, almost so that he lost sight of the big Indi'n.

As he saw the Cheyenne and Arapaho make his move on Chesney— and what a bold beautiful move it was—the angel being caught a glimpse of Styx. He was close enough to put his wing in harm's way. This beautiful wing deflected Styx's bullet from going straight into White Buffalo's chest. By first going through the big boy's arm, it slowed down enough to lodge into his thick chest muscle instead of his heart. The angel was thinking, *The Lord works in such mysterious ways,* as he finished off the last of the terrible stragglers.

CHAPTER SIXTEEN

"LOOKS LIKE WE'RE GOING TO get a little bit of moist. Well, make that a whole lot of moist," said an ol' black man to J.E.T. as he entered a QuikTrip convenience store on Garnett, just South of Highway 51 in Tulsa.

"You know, this storm might even bring some hailstones," the ol' man stated, not knowing if J.E.T. had heard him the first time.

"You might be right. I got caught in a downpour this morning. This one's picking up too; it might even get worse. Looks like we both might be in here for a while," J.E.T. said as the small talk grew.

"This is strange weather for this time of year," the old man said, as he winced when it thundered and lightning crashed nearby.

"Let me get you a cup of coffee and a peach pie, sir. Go ahead and have a seat. We'll sit a spell." J.E.T. turned away, not waiting for his answer.

"You know, there's something about a Dr. Pepper; it just tastes better in Oklahoma," J.E.T. exclaimed, not really thinking he would get a response from the store clerk. As he turned and gave the nice old black man a smile, he noticed out of the corner of his eye that about five, maybe half a dozen greasers were hustling through the store's door, trying to get out of the weather. J.E.T. thought, *If I didn't know any better, these must be the Crisco Kids,* and laughed to himself.

J.E.T. walked through the greasers and they looked him up and down as he went to sit with the old gentleman. As they talked, J.E.T. could tell that the boys' rowdiness wasn't going to subside anytime soon. And his spurs jingled.

"*Mojado,* I think it's about time you did some community service," the apparent leader said to the store clerk.

J.E.T. stood up and said, to no one in particular, "Oh, hey, no," on his way over to the ill-advised gathering. "Amigo, here's my phone. You to go over there to the end of the magazine rack. In a minute you're going to call 911," J.E.T. firmly said to the ol' black man, never taking his eyes off of the bad boys. "Tell the operator there are six bad guys and three civilians. Make that two civilians and one deputy U.S. marshal."

"And there's going to be trouble," the greaser added, finishing what J.E.T. was saying.

As J.E.T. got a little closer to the counter, he could hear the misfits' *patrón* whisper, "Give me all of the money."

The rancid gang was so focused on the clerk, only one of the six saw J.E.T. before he got about six feet from them.

"Guys, if you want trouble, meet me outside in five minutes. If I'm not there, start without me," J.E.T. said, rednecking them. This only made them more incensed, but J.E.T. thought it was funny and he chuckled to himself again.

"Stop right there," the gang's *jefe* almost shouted, because J.E.T. had surprised him. "And where did the old Negro man go?"

"It doesn't matter where he went, but I'm going to tell you and your friends this store just became real inconvenient for you," J.E.T. said calmly.

A quick right hand brought out a stiletto knife from the leader of the pack and it was going right toward J.E.T.'s throat.

With mongoose-like reflexes, J.E.T. took a half step back and grabbed the knife-wielding hand. This move got the greaser off balance. Then, J.E.T. stepped back toward him and made the leader do a quick quarter turn, which put the *jefe's* back against the store counter.

J.E.T. didn't stop there. The right arm of this bad guy was around his own neck and J.E.T.'s follow-through drove the blade of the knife into the store's countertop. This put the desperado in a very painful position because all the while J.E.T. had kept hold of the mean one's right hand and placed his left foot against the *jefe's* right foot, so that the bad guy was locked in a spine numbing, leg tingling predicament.

This move put J.E.T. in the perfect position to do some damage to the greaser farthest away from him. As J.E.T. had spun around the pretzeled leader, he switched hands and was now holding the bad *hombre's* hand with his right hand. He gave a nose-flattening back fist and a *pelota*-splitting blow to the bad lad. The boy fell on the floor, not knowing which part of his body to hold because with these blows, he would be out of his comfort zone for a long time.

One of the lowlife thugs was directly to J.E.T.'s left. He received a sharp side kick to the abdomen as he was pulling his fist back to blindside J.E.T.

This kick landed him in the Hostess rack. He then bounced back toward J.E.T. and J.E.T. was there to meet him with a roundhouse kick to the neck. This brachial stun knocked out the assailant long before his chin hit the floor.

As the snack rack fell on the would-be robber, J.E.T. wryly said, "Hey, Cupcake, Ding Dong."

The *tres bandoleros* that were left got a bright idea and started to attack J.E.T. all at the same time. Wrong move.

This attack was nothing a little aikido randori couldn't handle. Every move made by these hoodlums was quickly countered and throughout the fight J.E.T. never let go of the leader of the pack's hand.

The greasers were getting tired now and very beaten. Well, J.E.T. hadn't had this much fun in some time so he wasn't quite ready to finish them off just yet. But now they were only coming at him one at a time.

Several times, the crew had accidentally hit their own boss with the different weapons they had. That was until J.E.T. disarmed them. He then thought that now was the time to finish them off.

To the first one that came toward him, J.E.T. gave a good old-fashioned front kick to the solar plexus. This sent the groupie member halfway across the store into the magazine rack, where he found a great resting place by the Good Housekeeping magazines.

The next *mal muchacho* thought he saw daylight as J.E.T. recoiled from the front kick that sent his partner across the store.

With a swing from a tire iron that was like an Ichiro infield base hit, the bad *hombre* saw his opening. What he didn't see was the opening he had left for J.E.T. J.E.T.'s left hand landed a palm strike on the whiskered chin of the bad guy so that you could hear his teeth crack.

What was once daylight for him was now lights out, with no night light for comfort.

The last banger thought he had a trick up his sleeve when he went to pull out a gun from behind his denim jacket. He felt it was time to take out this one-man demolition crew.

No sooner had he started to reach inside his jacket than J.E.T. knew what was going to come out.

He had seen the revolver when the banger came into the store and the wind blew his jacket open. Everything started to slow down for J.E.T. Everyone's movements turned to slow motion, except for J.E.T.'s. Knowing he couldn't reach him with his foot, J.E.T. saw his next option.

He didn't want to let go of the number one bad guy, not just yet. The bind he had him in was pure agony.

J.E.T. reached back behind himself with his left hand. There was a parasol tube next to the *jefe* and he pulled one out. He swung it and grabbed the last bad guy's wrist with the hook before he was able to grab his gun. With a quick pull. the bad guy was on his way toward J.E.T. Then there was a crushing blow from an elbow that seemed to come out of nowhere. Before he could gather himself and even attempt to stop his momentum, J.E.T.'s elbow was right there waiting for him. *Bandolero* number six was hit so hard with J.E.T.'s elbow it crushed the orbital eye socket. J.E.T. knew the guy was going to look like the Boston Red Sox's Tony C. for a long, long time. The Crisco Kid fell to the floor right there and he wasn't getting up anytime soon, just like the rest of his *muchachos*.

J.E.T. had been holding up the mini mob's don for a while now. With the rest of the gang disposed of, he stepped off of Number One's foot and let go of the hand that was still curled around the knife handle. The bad guy was so beat up from his own men and so cramped from being in this position, he stiffly slid off the counter and crumbled to the floor.

"*Señor* Clerk, do you think you can find some duct tape or electrical tape and we'll wrap these guys up?" J.E.T. asked with a little grin and not a drop of sweat to be found. "First, we'll start with the number one Ding Dong (J.E.T. pointed to the leader), then number three Twinkie. Before you know it, we'll have all these cupcakes packaged together."

"Sir, were you able to contact Tulsa's finest?" J.E.T. asked the ol' gentleman.

"Alls I got was static on this phone," the ol' gentleman replied.

"Well, must be because of the weather," J.E.T. exclaimed.

Just then the power went out and the emergency lights came on.

"I got to get these boys tethered up, then all we can do is wait," J.E.T. said to the clerk and the ol' gentleman, not really looking for a response. Needing to talk to the sergeant but not being able to, he knew precious time would be slipping away—time needed to catch Del Rio before he did any more damage.

"Go ahead, finish your pie and coffee. I'll be there as soon as these boys are wrapped up," J.E.T. said to his new ol' friend.

It got darker as a storm grew, as the hail came and the sound became deafening...

CHAPTER SEVENTEEN

BEFORE ZAR AND J.E.T. WERE even close to the QuikTrip store, ZAR recognized the outline of an old comrade and Guardian.

This fellow angel's name was GEPE (pronounced *jeep*). He seemed almost as big and shapely as an armored Hummer. He wasn't as tall as J.E.T. or as brutally handsome; he just looked brutal. This block of a celestial being was about six feet two inches, with a square body that was about two feet thick. This was the design from which the Lord had made Paul "Mr. America" Anderson.

GEPE was Mr. Johnson's, guardian angel. GEPE loved being Mr. Johnson's angel, even at his ripe old age of eighty-six. Mr. Johnson loved going to church, reading his Bible and singing the old spiritual songs—Andraé Crouch being his favorite—and baseball. Mr. Johnson loved life but he loved the Lord more. This was such a privilege, being Mr. Johnson's angel.

At this stage of Mr. Johnson's life, he was still attacked quite often and from every angle. Today was only a little bit different because ZAR and J.E.T. were there and they were on the Lord's side, along with Mr. Johnson's.

GEPE didn't go out to meet ZAR; he waited until ZAR came into the convenience store. He didn't get very far from Mr. Johnson now, maybe ten feet at the most.

Not much of a talker, this Guardian of few words. But he always looked forward to the visits or battles he and ZAR shared.

After a quick greeting the two celestials majestically stood watch, then simultaneously turned their heads, ZAR to his left and GEPE to his right. Without turning their heads back, they glanced at each other and a steely grin came across both their faces as dark, shadowy figures started seeping in from the badlands.

You can't tell that GEPE enjoys the visit with ZAR, but you can sure tell he loves the war with him. That's what they are—battle born. From their beginning when the Son of God assigned them to their vocation, it was "love at first fight" for these warriors.

The Son instilled in each of his warriors the skills he knew they would need. He loved training them on how to fight and how to battle the powers and principalities of this world's Prince of Darkness.

As the spirits of Fear, Alcohol, Confusion, Turmoil, and many more came onto the property of the Quick Trip store, ZAR didn't waste any time greeting them with a "holy hit." GEPE was chomping at the bit, waiting for the demon thugs to get close since he wasn't going to leave Mr. Johnson's side.

ZAR decided to go hands-on to start the battle. He was going to leave his sword in its scabbard if at all possible, just for the fun of it. These first pesky dropouts weren't major players but there were quite a few of them. As always, ZAR took on the lead character of these speed demons. It always seemed like the spirit of Alcohol's unit led the way. It didn't matter to ZAR who led the way, to him it was "first come, first served."

"Whoa, you smell like a brewery. Your eyes are still red since the last time I saw you. Make sure you hit the right one, since you're seeing two of me," ZAR teased the smelly demon.

There had to be about twenty of these leeches. ZAR's speed with one burst of his wings caught the leader off guard, again. ZAR was at his blind side so fast that the demon was taking hits and all he could do was try, and I mean try, to cover up, the blows were coming so fast.

After ZAR did a quick dispatch of the first ghoul, he set his sights on the next five or so. He didn't give too much thought to which of the losers he would finish up with, since he knew GEPE was going to want to get into the action.

ZAR kind of toyed with these five. Again, he came in on their blind side. His speed seemed to always catch them off guard. This time he smacked the farthest one with his left wing—what a blow! This drove him into the next demon, which in turn drove him into the next, then the next and then the last of the five. ZAR wrapped the spirits up tight with both wings and squeezed them as if they were a machaca burrito from Roberto's.

ZAR held and squeezed them long enough that it just sucked the energy out of them. This was ZAR'S "black hole" technique.

By this time, the greasers had got to the counter and ZAR had given J.E.T. the jingle.

Now the darksiders saw Mr. Johnson, but with tunnel vision, so they didn't see GEPE. GEPE these days had changed his weapon of choice. Yeah, he still carried the sword but with having to stay so close to Mr. Johnson he had incorporated the bo staff too, probably in the last twenty years or so of Mr. Johnson's life.

GEPE brought out the staff and it seemed to come to life. It didn't matter which hand he used—it was just pure skill that only the Son can teach.

GEPE's first blow sent one demon straight down. His face hit the floor in what seemed like the same instant the bo staff struck the back of his head. Flying one second, down for the count the next.

As the next two spirit bangers were about to harass Mr. Johnson, GEPE spun like a whirlwind and the staff smashed the ribs of the one on the left. Then GEPE whirled around and smashed the ribs of the one on the right in the same place. When these two spirits crashed into each other it seemed like they had got hit at the exact same time as well.

GEPE continued spinning the bo staff with his left hand, waiting on the next contestant or contestants to enter his forbidden zone. Just then, ZAR grabbed a demonic spirit in each hand and threw them GEPE's way. GEPE obliged ZAR and caught the first on the left under the arm with the staff and drove him into the other spirit.

Now GEPE knew these two were entangled and he made the staff spin these demons head over heels about five times until he threw them away like the garbage that they were. The pinwheel pair were out of the fight for the rest of the afternoon.

"Nice, GEPE, they look like a couple of snow demons," ZAR said with the utmost approval as the demons were flailing around in spasms.

No need in stopping that bo staff now, ZAR thought, so he directed, and not so gently, the next four spirit villains towards GEPE.

GEPE's bo staff never missed a beat, literally! It could have been White Dragon style or Ninjutsu or Wing Chun, but whatever style he chose, they were all taught by the Son.

A little flash came on GEPE as he spun the bo staff over his head. Then he threw a between-the-leg spin into it, reminiscent of the young Warrior III yoga pose, right into the vertical backspin that ended up in his left hand. GEPE's not right- or left-handed, he's just destructive whichever hand he uses. So graceful for a full-figured body, yet so lethal.

GEPE faked a strike to the closest villain, which caused the villain's hands to cover his face. This allowed the other maniacs to get within striking distance. Then came the horizontal backspin. Of course, the ghouls weren't ready for the "Bo." They had caught up to their partner just as GEPE thought they would.

The first strike came from the right side. GEPE spun the staff in front of him to a horizontal position. With the ogres right on him, he gave the bo staff an uppercut motion that landed squarely under the chins of these demons. As if that didn't hurt enough, GEPE went into another vertical backspin so that when he came out on the other side, he let the momentum of the staff carry him up about three feet off the floor with the staff horizontal above the evil spirits' heads.

They were still so stunned by the uppercut that they didn't see the impending blow coming from above them. When the staff came down on the backs of their heads, GEPE drove them into the floor as he had with the first demon that had dared to wander into Mr. Johnson's zone.

GEPE saw that was eleven down and nine to go—but who's counting—as he anticipated the next hellions' arrival.

The next group were a little hesitant to attack either ZAR or GEPE, but they did anyway. Well, their hesitancy cost them precious time because ZAR was on them so fast it was like he had jet propulsion.

Now he used the same tactic he had with the previous five he had taken out. Only this time he threw these five to GEPE, who was eagerly awaiting their arrival.

ZAR proceeded to give the last four "the business." As he approached them, they were in a line. With his right hand he faked a punch to the second imp on the left. Well, the first imp on the left was caught off guard with that fake and received a side kick from ZAR to the left outer thigh. With this size sixteen foot he felt like he had been struck with the Bambino's thirty-six-inch, forty-six-ounce bat. He was out of the game. In fact, it looked like he would be on the disabled list for an extended period of time.

The imp he had faked was still covered up, with both arms covering his head. ZAR obliged this one with several punches to his floating ribs. The imp flew backward and just rolled up into a heap.

As for the next two, ZAR faked an upper block with his right arm to the clown on the left and, with another devastating sidekick, kicked the inner thigh of the last one on the right. The demon's leg went out from under him and he went into the splits. He wasn't about to get up anytime soon.

This group was from the spirit of No Confidence. That's why they were so hesitant to get aggressive in the fight. ZAR said to the lead demon, "Come on, you can do it, you've only been at this for how long now?"

"Shut up, ZAR," the embarrassed demon sheepishly said.

So, this last of the four demons decided he didn't want any of ZAR all by himself, but he had made his mind up too late. ZAR saw those arms still up covering his head and his rapid-fire body shots took this one out.

GEPE was in the middle of his one-to-five beatdown. This unit must have been the Cocky Spirit group. They came at GEPE with their hands down and their chins out, just begging GEPE to hit them. That was all the mistake GEPE needed.

GEPE thought, *If you want me to hit your chin first, I'll certainly accommodate your request.* He went right into a helicopter spin with the staff and then back to a hoop dance overhead palm spin.

This caught the dangerlings off guard because when GEPE got out of the overhead palm spin, he came across with the staff and hit the first three on his right, right on the chin. He then did a figure eight twice in front of him and when he stopped, he came across and hit the last two on their chins. As usual with GEPE's skills, he always hit the sweet spot and they fell like dominoes, or is it "demonoes."

Now there were two piles of these maniacs and they looked like dirty laundry lying about. One was out in the middle of the store's parking lot where ZAR had "Takin' Care of Business" and the others were strewn in the ten- to fifteen-foot range around Mr. Johnson that GEPE had easily created.

ZAR and GEPE would stay there until their men left the store. As ZAR looked at GEPE, he thought of the last battle they had been in together. It was near Fort Duchesne, in the Battle of the Monongahela, when GEPE was young George Washington, the bullet-proof president's, Guardian. Even though ZAR was assigned to protect Chief Attakullakulla during this time, GEPE needed ZAR that day...

CHAPTER EIGHTEEN

POWER HAD BEEN RESTORED AND the mess had been cleaned up at the inconvenient store by Tulsa's finest. J.E.T. was now able to talk to Sergeant Fred but the news wasn't as good as he had hoped for.

"That storm that came through here crapped out our equipment, again. Dadgummit!" Sergeant said as he got more torqued off than he was before.

"So, it's been about six and a half hours now, J.E.T. They did find the Power Wagon truck just down the road from the jail. Did you find anything at the house? They're off 71st Street," Fred asked J.E.T., not knowing that Tulsa P.D. hadn't made it to the house yet.

"Cuz, I haven't made it to the house yet either. Stopped off at a QuikTrip, was riding out the weather when some Ponyboy wannabes came in and got more than they asked for. They forgot to bring Darry, Dallas and Soda Pop!" J.E.T. said, halfway grinning.

"Okay!! So what's the plan now?" Sergeant said, knowing exactly what J.E.T. was referencing about the greasers. "Unless you think you can find some evidence of where they're going, fine, but they're long gone," he said matter-of-factly.

"Well, Cuz, we know now that they're headed west," J.E.T. said before the sergeant interrupted him.

"J.E.T., this just came in over the wire. An Indian Smoke Shop in Clinton got robbed and a security guard was shot. Two guys did the robbery with one of them matching Del Rio's description. Also, there was a possible third one as the getaway driver." Sergeant's voice got a little excited with all of this. "I'll be dadgummed, but no description of the vehicle they were driving."

"With what little info we have from the phone calls, we do know that his cousin Isis is from Arizona, you know what town she's from?" J.E.T. asked Fred, hoping for the information.

"Sergeant, get Muskogee P.D.'s evidence tech to go over the Power Wagon and run all of their prints. Let's see who this third guy is," J.E.T. said. "I'm going to 'pop smoke,' as one of my favorite sergeants used to say. I'll head to Concho and reach out to the BIA at the Cheyenne and Arapaho Tribes. All of the officers I worked with are either retired or gone, but I'll see if they got anything for us and see how the guard is doing. Talk to you in a little bit," J.E.T. said as he hung up the phone

J.E.T. thought for a moment, *They've been gone these six and a half hours, so far going west and the cousin Isis is in Arizona somewhere. Northern, southern, Arizona—where is she?* This question grew in his mind. *There is no way I'm going to catch this wild bunch in a car. I'll get a late flight out of Oklahoma City. But first I'll head over to Concho and see what information the Bureau of Indian Affairs has on the robbery.*

J.E.T. looked over his rental car and thought, *Huh, no hail damage? Good thing because that would have cost me even more valuable time.*

He turned the radio on after he got the reservation for his flight. Knowing of no Phil and Brent on KMOD, especially "Roy D.," at that time of day, he turned it over to some preaching music on KXOJ. *Listen to that,* he thought, *old-school Rez Band "Reach of love." Wow, that brings back memories.* And he settled in for his two-hour trip to Concho BIA.

It was almost 8 p.m. when he arrived at Concho. He thought to himself, *My old stomping grounds, where I cut my teeth.* Just before he got out of the car, Fred called.

"Talk to me Cuz," J.E.T. said, needing some good info.

"J.E.T., I just got some intel on the wire that there was another robbery in Groom, Texas, but this time with two murdered and one badly injured. I talked to the P.D. there. They said that another one probably won't make it either. Pretty gruesome, they said." Sergeant added, "There was a Buick left there, not a truck, so the P.D. is trying to get prints even as we speak. Who knows if the car is theirs, but we should find out soon where they got it. There are several used car dealers in the area, so at this time we don't know if they took one of those cars or carjacked one. Groom P.D. is trying to call all of their car dealers to check their inventory to see if we can figure out what they're driving now."

"Well I'm here at Concho now. I'll talk to these officers and see if they got any more 411. Hey Cuz, I'm catching a flight out of OKC as soon as possible. These hoodlums are way too far ahead of me to catch. These guys are getting more violent as they go. So we're pretty sure, and I feel, that they're going to Arizona, just haven't figured out where yet. North, south, east or west? I'll fly into Phoenix and hopefully we'll get some good intel by then. *Chooch,* there's going to be a lot of carnage by the time we get these guys," J.E.T. said, in an almost a prophetic statement, "isn't there, Cuz?"

All Sergeant could say was, "Yes, there is."

As J.E.T. walked up to the BIA office, the light in the parking lot was out. Just then he heard and saw an owl as it flew past the office lights. J.E.T. paused for a second, thinking of the superstitions that go with an owl: If you hear an owl, someone is going to get hurt; if you see an owl, someone is going to die. It made him pause for a moment before he went into the office, thinking about that old superstition.

The only news J.E.T. got from C&A was that their security guard was going to make it. He'd be out for a while, but he'd make it. J.E.T. thought, *Well at least some good news for a change.*

As J.E.T. got on the plane, the skies didn't seem as friendly as usual, even when he flew on Con-Air. He could only wonder what the next victims of Del Rio had in store for them.

When J.E.T. arrived at Sky Harbor, he called Sergeant as soon as he got into the terminal.

"Any word on the hooligans?" J.E.T. asked.

"After Groom, it went dark—a few murders, well, six murders to be exact. These have to be the luckiest greasers alive; no one has got any description of their cars and they haven't been pulled over by any law enforcement agency," Sergeant Williams said, hating to give J.E.T. the bad news. "P.S., by the way, the murders were in Tucumcari and Defiance. So, east side and west side of New Mexico."

"Okay Fred, those losers are in Arizona now. I can feel it. Thanks for the help, I'll get ahold of you soon. Be safe, Cuz!" J.E.T. said, sincerely. "Oh, and by the way, tell Sheriff Seeban I'll catch him next time I'm in town. I'm sure he has a new car or motorcycle that he needs to give me a ride in or take for a ride," J.E.T. requested.

"You as well, Cuz, and I'll tell the sheriff," Fred said as he hung up the phone.

CHAPTER NINETEEN

AS J.E.T. DROVE DOWN THE road toward Concho, ZAR stood on the trunk of J.E.T.'s car and kept a keen eye out.

There weren't a whole lot of skirmishes on the way, but there were a few. Every so often, a prince of the town they were going through would want to challenge ZAR. In turn, ZAR would oblige the spirits, dispatching them very quickly so as not to get too far from J.E.T. Little towns, little princes.

When they got to Concho, ZAR had his work cut out for him. The superstitions that surrounded the tribal land just made the whole place dark, except for the folks who believed and worshiped the Great One and his son. These folks lit their area up like beacons.

There's Veho (the Spider Trickster), Axxea (the horned serpent—it menaces travelers), Enemy Dwarfs (dangerous little people), Two Face (with a face front and back) and many other superstitious and folklore demons that just try to deceive good natives.

ZAR wasn't about to go hands-on only this go-around; his sword was in his hand long before he hit the tribal land. He moved to the front of the car, kicked himself from the car, spread his wings and was in battle mode as they turned off Northwest Expressway onto Highway 81, the road that leads to Concho.

ZAR thought to himself, *my old battlegrounds,* as they approached Black Kettle Boulevard.

ZAR's sword was on display as they entered this familiar land. He dipped down to the ground and dragged the tip of his sword. When he brought it back up, the fireball on the end of the sword lit up that darkness like a continuous bolt of lightning.

ZAR had to fight off the demon on Black Kettle Boulevard that likes to sit in the back seat of cars traveling through, just before you get to the BIA office.

ZAR had to fight him many of the times J.E.T. had gone through this area and tonight was no exception. The attack came fierce, but as per usual, ZAR was ready for it.

When this demon approached ZAR, ZAR could see some of the old battle scars he had given the demon eighteen or so years earlier. ZAR looked at him and said, "Come get some," and the fight was on.

Well, sort of. Did the evil spirit not see ZAR's fireball, did he forget the times ZAR had used it on him and his rudimentary ghoul comrades, or was he just overconfident?

The demon had two swords and a lot of so-called "friends." It didn't matter to ZAR.

As they came out of the darkness into the light, they were temporarily blinded by the light of the fireball ZAR had on the tip of the sword. In turn, ZAR only had to start out with the basics of sword fighting. A simple front step and an overhead strike knocked the demon to the ground, not to mention the burn from the fireball that he got. The demon was thinking, *It's all fun and games until someone brings a fireball to a sword fight,* as he lay there licking his wounds, literally.

Now this took ZAR away from J.E.T. as J.E.T. headed toward the BIA office. The demons were coming in droves now, so much that it was like a black hole just sucking these demons toward him. The fiends' appetite for destruction overwhelmed them so much they couldn't see that ZAR was discarding them in burning heaps as they were coming in. What had started out as basic sword fighting, well, ZAR had to step it up several notches.

This display of skill from ZAR really was almost unprecedented. Very few of the other Guardians had this skill. The assailants came from the eight counties of that reservation and a few more demons from the Comanche and Apache tribes joined in as well. But they also met a beatdown that they hadn't experienced for quite a while.

The maniacs were trying to tag in and out of the fight, but as each one looked to another imp to help out, they were discarded onto the heap along the side of the road. So they got tagged in, but they were definitely "tapped out."

As this fight roared on, J.E.T. had made it to the P.D., got some information, and by now was on his way to Will Rogers Airport. ZAR had seen him go by an hour or so earlier. ZAR elevated the fight so that the farther J.E.T. got from him he could at least still see him. With those twenty-five miles or so from Concho to Will Rogers, ZAR had to get up close to a mile in the air with the fight to keep J.E.T. in his line of sight.

With J.E.T. on the plane, ZAR had to send as many of these wraiths into the screaming pile that he could. But now was the time to catch the next nonstop flight to Sky Harbor. So, with a burst from his wings, ZAR was riding on the tail of the plane, looking in on J.E.T. and waiting on the next fight—'cause he knew it would be here soon— while relishing the battle he'd just had, taking out some old foes like it was yesterday. If days matter to him, then it had been a good day, doing the LORD's work.

CHAPTER TWENTY

"CARHOP, WE NEED TO FIND 4024 West Palm Lane," Styx more demanded than stated. "When we get to Isis' house, don't either one of you tell her about the trip here," he again demanded, not wanting Isis to know about the murders.

"Carhop, be on the lookout for a sedan that you think might be pretty fast, that we can pick up in a couple of days," Styx instructed.

"Okay," Carhop responded. Beat from the trip, Carhop was really tired. He had driven most of the way. But what was bothering him most was seeing the faces of all of the people Styx had killed along the way. He couldn't get them out of his mind. Just being around Styx was like a black hole to him; Styx just sucked the energy out of him.

"Case, Isis is supposed to have the rest of the crew there," Styx said as he took another hit of the blast, even though he'd been up for about thirty-six hours. "So, with us, Isis and the four other cousins, that's eight of us," Styx said, just thinking out loud. "That's a good number for what we are going to do." Again, thinking out loud.

When they arrived at Isis' house, she went out to meet them. Hugs for Case and Styx, and she met Carhop. "Let's go in the house, guys, and you'll see the rest of the cousins," Isis said, excited to see them.

Inside the house the four cousins got up and greeted Styx and Case. These four had some size, unlike Styx and Case. They were between six feet two inches and six feet four inches, with about 230 to 240 pounds on their thick frames. Styx had kind of forgotten how big his kinfolk were, but it didn't matter. If he would have been only five feet two inches, he would have still been the *jefe*.

After a little small talk, Styx got to the point and asked Isis if everything was in place. She said it was and that he didn't have to worry about anything. Styx was wondering why Isis wasn't at work so he asked her, "By the way cousin, why aren't you at work?"

"I took the afternoon off. I told my boss that I had a doctor's appointment, so it's cool!" she exclaimed. "I'm getting excited about this. That land was in our family for a long time and then it was taken away from us. They had no right to it," She continued.

"You know, Isis, we all got done dirty. We all deserve this," Styx said, playing on her emotions, not really caring if anyone there but him got all this ill-gotten booty.

"Isis, take us over there to your job. You're going to stay in the car while myself and Case go inside and check it out. Do you have a drawing of the place?" he asked her.

To which Isis said, "Yes."

"And the guys here have already looked the drawing over?" Styx asked her.

Again, she said, "Yes."

"Good. Isis, you'll ride in the back seat of my car with Case. Myself and Carhop will ride in front, while you guys take your van over there. But don't park in front of the place. Go by it and park on the next block and stay in the van until we leave Isis' job and pass you by. While you're there, look around the area and keep mental notes of which are the busiest stores or shops around, then we'll talk about it when we get back. Head east to Highway 60, that's Superstition Freeway, then get off on South Superstition Mountain Drive. That's Three Wells. Let's go," Styx said, not waiting for a response.

When Styx and Case got inside the building, they started to count employees as they tried to be inconspicuous. Case grabbed one of their forms and pretended to fill it out while Styx cased the place. After they got the 411 they needed, they left the building.

They drove by their cousins and stopped about a block and a half down the road. As the cousins pulled up beside them, Styx said, "Okay boys, let's get back on Superstition and drive about ten miles south of here to make sure there is no road construction. Then we'll meet back at Isis' place."

By the time they got to Isis' house, Styx had the plan pretty much laid out. He gave everyone their assignments and reiterated that this money had always belonged to them anyway, because it was literally stolen from their family years ago, all the while knowing it was all a lie. He had them eating out of the palm of his hand and believing every last lie he told.

Whoever said blood is thicker than water never met Styx. He could care less about his kin; he just wanted the money....

Styx pulled his big cousins aside and asked them if they had everything ready. By ready, he meant he wanted to see the firepower they were going to bring to the party.

In low voices, they told him that the "party favors" were there. Styx, not wanting Isis to know about the guns, sent her out to get them some dinner. He sent her to a place he had heard of that took its sweet time to get the orders ready.

When Isis was gone, the weapons came out. Styx asked his cousin, "Where'd you get these?"

With a smile on his face he professed, "South of the border, Baby."

With everyone in on the plan, Styx made sure that no one, absolutely no one, was to make it out of that building alive.

Carhop, wondering how he ever got to this place, said to himself, *I should be racing somewhere, but now I'm all mixed up with these murderers. My feet feel like they're in cement.*

Thursday morning brought excitement, fear, a heightened sense of greed, arrogance, nervousness, so many different feelings to each of these wannabe notorious gang members. Waiting until late afternoon was going to be very hard for them.

That evening, Carhop had ditched the car they came to town in. He picked up another inconspicuous one for the next couple of days that they were to be there.

"Carhop, go get that car that you've had your eye on for the last couple of days," Styx said, setting the plan into motion.

Carhop and Case took off. He had driven a few of these cars in the last couple of years in Tulsa and Broken Arrow. But this one reminded him of the one he drove in Broken Arrow. It brought back memories of flying down Weer Road, taking the back way to Coweta.

Carhop excitedly said to Case, "There it is," as they pulled up to the 1996 Impala SS dark cherry-red model.

"Okay Carhop, do your magic and let's get out of here," Case said as he looked around for a place to put the sedan they were in.

"Give me fifty-five to sixty seconds and I'll be in and we'll be out of here," Carhop said, getting more nervous by the second. Just like he said, he got in and within a minute was picking up Case where he had parked the other car.

"Let's get out of here!" Case ordered, almost shouting at Carhop.

Carhop was glad this had gone without a hitch as he drove back to the desperados' house, trying not to speed.

When they got back, Styx came out of the house and told Carhop, "So this is what you're going to get us out of there with. Not bad," half belittling and half commending him.

The three of them went back into the house for one last go-through of the plan. "I don't care why the Broward Copper Company wanted to bring their payroll to Isis' bank this week, but they did. And since they took our family's land years ago and our family didn't get a dime of the claim, then it's our right to get this money." As Styx spoke, they were all sitting there, thinking and murmuring, "Yeah! It's our money. We deserve it at all costs."

"Isis, are you sure there will be eight, maybe nine at the most, employees there and no security?" Styx asked, almost badgering Isis.

"Yes," Isis answered, wondering why he was questioning her again.

"Grab your bags and let's go. Remember, Isis, you're riding with me, Case and Carhop. You guys are going in the van," Styx directed his linebacker corps-looking cousins.

One of the cousins said, "Good thing it's not a minivan," very much meaning what he said.

As Carhop started the SS, the radio blared Van Halen's "DEAD or ALIVE, dead or alive." Styx, Case and Carhop looked at each other but didn't say a word. And the plan was set in motion!!

CHAPTER TWENTY-ONE

"HEY BRO'," J.E.T. SAID AS Whit answered the phone, "what's going on?"

"Just finishing up a project here. What's going on with you, Deputy Marshal?" Whit answered.

"Can we get together later this afternoon over at the diner, you know, the one by Paul's Drywall Supply and across the street from Polly's Pantry, there in Three Wells? I got to go back out of town this weekend, so we'll just have dinner later. Cool?" J.E.T. asked, trying to get their "bro' time" in.

"Yeah, sure. My project will be finished up and I'll see you there. I like that diner so, yeah, that's cool with me," Whit responded.

"I know you like your gizzards!" J.E.T. said, kind of playing.

As J.E.T. finished up his day at work he went over the schedule for his next pickup on Con-Air and had the details down for that. But what was on his mind all week was, *What happened to Del Rio and whoever was with him in Muskogee County's breakout? Why have there not been any more killings?* Not that he wanted any more, but since Monday the trail had been getting very cold.

Nothing had come back from cousin Fred about who Isis was, where she lived or what she did for a living, only that it was in Arizona. J.E.T. could only think of those car jackings and robberies, how they became more violent the farther they got from Muskogee.

Next up for these hoodlums, J.E.T. felt like it was going to be more of a bloodbath than all the other crimes put together.

J.E.T. left the office and got home at about two. He went out to his garage and went through the full wooden dummy Wing Chun sets. He thought before he got started, *If you forget Wing Chun for a day, it will forget you for two days,* true to his white-haired sifu master. The dummy took its beating like a champ. That set not only would have made his sifu master proud, but he would have made Grandmaster as proud as well!

J.E.T. was also needing some riding time, to let all of this sink in. He put on his riding boots, shoulder holster with a compact Sig Sauer P245 snapped inside and an extra magazine. He threw a stiletto in his pocket, just to even it out. Wearing a black vest and a Thunder Mountain Harley t-shirt, he grabbed his jacket, ready for that desert air.

When he got back to the garage, as the door opened, he had already strapped on the jacket to the handlebars of his Phat-Tailed Deuce. He pushed the bike out, past the '70 cranberry red LS6 Chevelle SS. As he set out on his ride, he had about an hour and a half to kill. He said to himself, *Long live the long bike.*

The early December weather felt so good in Phoenix as he initially headed west. Then he turned south and eventually went back toward the east. The Big Deuce's motor sang its lonesome song as J.E.T. thought of when he used to ride with his oldest and best friend Zane and his double cousin Artemis. The miles they rode together really cemented their relationship. They probably rode 45,000 miles together throughout their youth.

As J.E.T. turned off of Highway 79 onto Superstition Highway he was riding northwest. As he went through the gears he looked west, and what a sight to behold! This had to be the most beautiful pre-sunset he had ever seen.

There were so many colors displayed there. The deep reds, transitioning to the oranges and yellows. The black and the grays that the sun's rays couldn't get through hung in the sky like a furnace bellowing out its sulfur gases, smoke and ash. J.E.T. was almost surprised that there were no embers flying out of this masterpiece.

Even with the Big Deuce's throaty exhaust, he could hear some rumblings of thunder coming from the awesome display of this bonfire in the sky.

All of a sudden, J.E.T. felt that the burning sky was bringing a sense of destruction. He wondered where those thoughts came from.

As J.E.T. neared the exit there to Three Wells he started downshifting, recalling that the diner was just a couple of blocks away.

When he turned down the street with the diner, he could see Paul's Drywall Supply and Polly's Pantry. There it was and there was Whit's car, sitting in front of the diner.

Whit's never late, J.E.T. thought, pulling up alongside that classic muscle 1969 Z/28 Rally Sport. By the time he had put the kickstand down with those size eleven Bowden black harness boots, Whit was already outside the diner to meet him.

"Hey Bro', how you doing?" J.E.T. asked Whit as they gave each other a hug.

"Just enjoying my days off," Whit exclaimed, since he just retired because of Huntington's disease. He continued, "You want to see my latest project?" with a grin on his face.

"Sure, where is it?" JET asked, wondering what he was talking about.

Whit walked over to the front of that black-with-white-stripes Z/28, pulled on the hood latch and raised the flat hood to show J.E.T. the new motor he had put in.

"What we got here is a ProCharged, cross ram, 302DZ that my buddy Leo and I put together. That and we also put in a Gear Vendors overdrive. As of right now Deputy, this is a three-mile-a-minute-car," Whit said, matter-of-factly. "I also put in a couple of suspension parts as well. It ain't scared."

J.E.T. looked and looked at what Whit had done to the Z. "Bro', you remember when I was thirteen and you were fourteen and I was working at the Husky station at the end of town?"

"Sure do," Whit said.

"And McMahan stopped right there in front of the station. I called for you and David. With his uncorked headers and slicks, his '69 Z/28 shot out of there like an electric slot car. Bro, that's been my favorite car ever since, and you got one! Start it up. Let's hear this beast!"

When Whit started up the hot rod he said, "302 on the Richter scale," with a big smile on his face. After a few more minutes, he shut the car off. They went into the diner and reminisced about those younger days, as they saw time slip away.

Just then Van Halen's "Finish What You Started" came on the speakers in the diner. Without hesitation, Whit said jokingly (speaking of Eddie Van Halen), "He's above average." He added, "But he ain't no Bonnie Raitt," again jokingly. J.E.T. laughed like usual.

This very attractive waitress, all five foot two inches, 106 pounds or so of her, with straight dark brown hair, in a bob cut with some spike on the top and dark eyes, brought them their menus and took their drink orders. She had a figure so nice she would have looked great in a gunny sack, much less her waitress dress. She was probably in her mid to late twenties. But when J.E.T. looked at her, he knew he was in trouble!

Whit went for the root beer and J.E.T. just water for now, while both of them had to make themselves not stare at this gorgeous young lady.

When she said she would be back with their drinks and get their orders, Whit and J.E.T. were kind of speechless, until after she had come back and left with their orders.

J.E.T. said, "Okay, where were we?" as they both grinned, thinking of this lovely lady. "You probably haven't been training with all the work you put into that black beauty."

"Not as much as usual, but I got in a couple of forms today," Whit said.

"Bro', do you remember when we started Wing Chun?" Whit asked.

"Oh yeah," J.E.T. replied. "That was cool, just down the street when we lived at Apache Circle when we were kids. Walk down to sifu's house, get our training in and go home. Man, you couldn't beat that."

"Yeah, we got that Kung Fu action in," Whit said, grinning.

"You know, Bro', it was always more natural for you than it was for me. Man, I still have to work at it," J.E.T. said proudly of his brother. "Then you go on and train at least four other styles of martial arts. You're a stud, Bro'."

After dinner, out came the dessert menu as per usual. Waitress Kari Ann brought them the chocolate cream pie that they ordered and sat down with them for a few minutes, as the diner was a little slow.

Several times during their dinner, J.E.T. would look toward the Three Wells Bank and Trust. What had seemed okay now seemed like something was out of place. But he couldn't put his finger on it.

As he was looking, he saw a blue panel van and the tail end of a deep cherry red car on the other side of it that hadn't been there before. J.E.T. looked at his watch and thought it was kind of busy for closing time at the bank.

"Bro', don't go anywhere. I need to run over here to the bank for a minute," J.E.T. told Whit.

"Why, what's up?" Whit asked.

"Ah, nothing. I'm just going over there and I'll be right back," J.E.T. replied. "Miss Kari Ann, please don't let my bro' leave; we still have some catching up to do," he said as he put $40 on the table, which included a healthy tip, and looked into those beautiful eyes.

Kari Ann said, "Yeah, sure," as J.E.T. got up and went out the door.

As he swung his leg over the Big Deuce, he paused and looked back toward the bank and fired up the bike. At that moment, J.E.T. could feel the sorrow, as if it were coming off the strings of Gilmour's number one Stratocaster.

When he rode toward the bank, how did he know that this town was in for some terrible agony?

CHAPTER TWENTY-TWO

WHILE J.E.T. WAS AT HIS office in the city, ZAR had been paying attention to a house on the other side of town. A lot of demons had been coming and going from that area over the past few days. They were there when he got back from his trip to Oklahoma but they hadn't been there when they left for Oklahoma.

ZAR just stood there, this savagely handsome, majestic being, with his hand resting on his sword, staring a hole through miles of space and the demons not aware that he was back in their neighborhood.

They were too far away for ZAR to do some of his Force Recon—about fifteen miles. ZAR would usually only go about five miles from J.E.T.'s side on recon missions.

Even though ZAR was fixated on the demonic activity, he wasn't oblivious to what J.E.T. was saying or doing. When he heard J.E.T. call Whit and set up their "bro' time," he thought it was always good to get together with the two of them, Whit and his Guardian.

Now that J.E.T. was on his way home, ZAR was looking at the area where all the demon activity was, with more of them coming in than going out. But they still didn't get close enough for ZAR to really see who and what was going on.

ZAR looked on with pride as J.E.T. was going through his wooden dummy sets. He wanted to tell J.E.T. that today he couldn't have done any better than J.E.T. had done.

ZAR remembered the beginning of this wooden dummy training and how the Son had put this into the hearts of men, how to train and fight for the good.

With J.E.T.'s long bike roaring down the road, ZAR would either stand on the back fender and scour the horizon or he would soar along with the bike.

During the trip, ZAR caught a half dozen or so rogue rebellions. It didn't take much to send these enemies belly-up on the desert floor.

As they neared Three Wells, ZAR could feel the presence of his spirit kind. In the middle of Three Wells, there they were, ASTRAL with Whit and three other warriors.

ASTRAL was this Guardian that had Hollywood leading-man good looks. The long brown hair flowed past his shoulders, maybe seven to eight inches down his back. Those blue eyes could pierce you if you were the enemy or they could embrace you if you were his friend. The tan skin showed off his capped shoulders and wide back. The tight waist gave way to some deep-cut thighs. If he were human, he would be five feet nine inches and about 195 pounds. The Guardians were quite the specimens from God and ASTRAL was no different. Most of the Guardians were not quick to smile, but when they did it was very sincere.

ZAR thought back to the time when they were Guardians of two of King David's Three Mighty Men.

ASTRAL was the Guardian for Jashobeam, and what a warrior he was. But through the ages he had become just as fond of and committed to Whit as he had been to Jashobeam on the day he killed 800 by himself, at one time, for King David.

ZAR and ASTRAL greeted each other, along with the three other Guardians there. All five of the Guardians were facing the bank when ZAR spoke, "A Rage!! There were tens of them in Oklahoma; now there are thousands of them here at the bank!" ZAR let the others know that he knew who this seditious bunch was.

Guardian ROBATO was there for a six-year-old boy at the old soda fountain, sitting on a stool at the counter.

ROBATO was the angelic being who stood right at six feet three inches. He had this straight blond Beatle-like hair style with hints of red in it, especially in his mustache. Now, ROBATO was slim and he was one of the exceptions because it seemed like he always had a smile on his face. If he were human you would wish everyone had a best friend like him because he just drew you in. But when it came time to ward his human subjects, he was so good with his hands he could carve or forge any opponent sent his way.

ZAR had some fond memories of ROBATO. Through the ages he'd had scuffles alongside this dedicated warrior.

ZAR had heard of the kind of servant and protector ROBATO had been with John, not only on the island of Patmos, but throughout his long life. Fighting alongside him was always a privilege.

These angels knew the demonic world would try anything to get to the Lord's children. They also knew that the young, weak, old and disabled were even more susceptible to demon attacks and bombardments.

Another Guardian in the room was AILIN. He was there to protect the six-year-old's widowed mother. She was sitting next to her son at the soda fountain as well. They were there just enjoying each other's company.

AILIN was all of six feet four inches tall, a medium-built Guardian. His face had this little-boy look to it. You would have thought he might have a chipped tooth like little boys get, he was so young looking. He was a quiet Guardian though, like many of them were. But if he were human, he would have been so thoughtful to the needs of his friends. This is what made him such a good Guardian, always so diligent with his squire's protection and service.

ZAR's thoughts ran back to a time when he had heard stories of AILIN and REGA and how they had fought side by side almost fifty years earlier in Korea.

There was a certain soldier who ended up in a prisoner-of-war camp. He was a seventeen-year-old who had gotten captured after only two weeks in country.

That he endured his three and a half years of brutality was nothing short of a miracle. After his capture, they took his boots during a bitterly cold Korean winter. The march to the first POW camp was so horrendous that if a prisoner fell, the North Koreans would kill him right there.

There was the time a dozen or so U.S. soldiers were put in a three and a half-foot to four-foot square bamboo cage and left there until their spines snapped. All but two of them made it.

Throughout the imprisonment, they continued to torture in unimaginable ways. Always if a prisoner fell or couldn't make it, he was killed. Then he was turned over to the Red Chinese and the torture was just as bad. Actually, it was worse.

Three and a half years of propaganda—that the Koreans and Red Chinese had captured the United States.

Three and a half years of raw rice and fish heads to eat.

Three and a half years of losing so much weight that at 100 pounds he was just a shell of a now-young man.

That he had aged thirty years physically in that three and a half years.

Three and a half years of no sleep, of betrayal without judgment, of teeth pulled out without anesthesia, of boils lanced instead of surgery.

Three and a half years!!!

BUT, but three things were certain: GOD LOVED this young man. His parents' steadfast prayer for their missing-in-action son. The comfort that the good Lord gave his mom—she knew that he was still alive during those three and a half years. When so many were dying or being killed around him, Almighty God was answering prayer.

Then there was AILIN and REGA for three and a half years. There was not one second that they weren't defending this young man with his incredible fortitude.

ZAR thought of the times when he was told that AILIN would put this young man's face in his hands and put his forehead against his forehead, just when it was almost over for this young man, and whisper, "Don't give up, brother. Your people are waiting for you. God loves you no matter what and your family loves you!"

Other times, while the battle was raging over this young warrior, REGA would sit down beside him, rest the young man's head on his shoulder, engulf him with his wings and whisper to him, "Brother, don't give up. I'm here for you. Just rest." And in those dire moments he was able to gain strength for another day, another hour or another minute.

Little did this warrior of a man know there was a beautiful young lady waiting for him back home. His picture was all she had seen of him, but it was love at first sight. And through her prayers as well, that this young man would make it through three and a half years of living hell.

When this young man made it back to the States, these majestic, fearsome, twosome beings didn't leave his side for the six months he was in the hospital. This young man's middle name even translates to majestic.

This was the end of REGA's special assignment, the day the young warrior got out of the hospital. He was left in great hands with the warrior AILIN until the day he passed, with two children he wasn't supposed to be able to have and four grandchildren. But before he passed, AILIN got to witness his squire give his heart to Jesus. Oh, happy day!!

The fourth guardian at the diner was REGA. This was an athletic looking angelic being! He was close to five feet eleven inches, with a muscular build that was nothing short of spectacular. If he were human his athleticism would have been on display with football skills, baseball skills, tennis skills, it wouldn't matter. When it came to this angel's personality, he was very humorous but also a type A individual.

If he told you something, he wasn't going to take no for an answer. Well, obviously he would be right since he'd almost seen it all. But he was another one you would be so thankful for if he were your friend. He was always there when another Guardian needed him, no questions, just ready to jump into the fight.

REGA was there as Kari Ann's Guardian. She'd had it pretty rough growing up. Her dad pretty much raised her and her siblings, due to an illness her mother had when she was very young. But this Guardian was able to send someone into her life who made her receptive to the love of Jesus while she was in her early to mid-twenties. And she had been following the Lord ever since.

REGA was known for directing a young boy through his adolescence after his father passed away when the boy was only five weeks old. Not much later, a stepfather abandoned the family. Young Billy, at ten years old, along with his brother, was sent to an orphans' home because of an impoverished mother.

This young man's athleticism became known and by the time he was twenty years old he was playing major league baseball. But after eight years in the big leagues, he turned down a lucrative baseball contract and got his start in the ministry at the local YMCA. That led to him becoming one of the biggest evangelists at the turn of the twentieth century—Billy Sunday.

Along with watching the demonic block party that all of the demons in Southern Arizona were invited to, ZAR was paying close attention to J.E.T. and how the bank had captured his curiosity.

So when J.E.T. told Whit he was going to the bank, it didn't surprise ZAR at all; he was actually kind of expecting it.

"Well, Motivators," ZAR said to the other warriors, "looks like we're going to meet and greet these usurpers, whether they like it or not!"

ZAR and REGA followed J.E.T. out the diner door as he was drawn to the bank. ZAR pointed out Styx to REGA. "That kid's made some bad choices since he left Muskogee County. He had maybe a few demons then, but look at him now—he's Hooked on Demonics! Thousands of demons going in and out of him. This is about to get empirical!" ZAR exclaimed, in his best Dennis Miller impersonation. "Yeah, this is about to become as real as it gets," REGA responded. "Maybe to them this is going to be as synthetic as it gets!"

So when J.E.T. fired up that big fat tire bike, the two warriors were already on their way to "The Rage."

CHAPTER TWENTY-THREE

WHEN THEY GOT IN THE SS, Case asked Styx, "You want one of these left-handed cigarettes?"

Styx just looked at him like he was an idiot and took out another hit of blast. By now, Styx had been up for days. He was going over his notes, reliving the killings that he had done on Route 66. It might as well have been Route 6 6 6, with what Styx had done.

As Carhop started the car, the radio was banging out "Highway to Hell, we're on the Highway to Hell." Carhop, trying to lighten the mood, said, "I thought we were going on Superstitious Highway." As he giggled, no one else did. Carhop pulled out a weakling and asked Isis if she wanted one.

She said, "I don't smoke, but thanks anyway."

The big boys pulled in behind them and after what seemed like forever, they were pulling up to the bank. "Isis," Styx questioned, "are you sure the copper mine payroll came to this bank today?"

Isis, getting perturbed and anxious, said, "Tim, I'm sure it's here, so quit asking!"

Styx's paranoia was kicking into high gear with all that blast he'd done and the days without sleep.

"Let's drive around back and Isis will see whose cars are there so we won't be surprised if any other employees show up," Styx said. He was thinking, *I'm the smartest man in the world,* as he sucked on a smootherette. He liked the way that Kool menthol tasted as he blew smoke rings, anticipating the heist.

Isis looked around, told Styx whom each car belonged to and when she was done, there were no new employees there to surprise them.

"Isis, you stay in the back of the car but leave it running. Carhop, Case, grab your bags," Styx said as he motioned for the big boys to come on over. "Okay, remember no one makes it out alive!" Styx reminded them.

"You two are going upstairs. You two are going to watch the people in the lobby and the front door. Carhop, you are going to cover the side door while Case and myself are going to take care of the clerks and the people near the vault."

All these thugs were wired up. All of their parents, except Carhop's, had done time or were doing time. So, when they put on their black ball caps, dark cheap sunglasses and bandanas up to their eyes, it felt natural to them.

They entered the bank quietly, to try and get in as far as possible before anyone had a chance to hit the alarms. They were able to get about fifteen feet inside before anyone noticed them. Then Styx started yelling instructions: "On the floor, except for the clerks." Then he yelled it again: "Get on the floor, except for the clerks!"

Styx knew there wasn't an alarm button upstairs, so he wasn't too worried about that. But the cousins ran up the stairs before anyone could call 911. What they found were a few employees, and one of them was the manager. They were quickly herded down the stairs to join the others.

"Okay boys, start your packaging!" Styx ordered. The brothers pulled out the packaging tape and started to tape hands and feet.

There was one *hombre* who looked like he could hold his own against a couple of these thugs. His fingers were a size twelve or thirteen and the rest of him matched his hands. Yeah, he was big! The brother who was going to tape up this *hombre* took one look at him and asked, in his best Southern twang and with a grin on his face, "Hey 'omber, you *muy macho* with a side of *muy malo?*"

The *hombre* yielded and as he was getting his hands tied behind his back, he was so stiff that he could barely put them together to be taped.

Just then the thug pulled out his switchblade and shoved it into the *hombre's* kidney. This turned him around and then the thug buried the blade into his femoral artery, just to watch him bleed out.

He cut a piece of tape and put it over the *hombre's* mouth just for the fun of it. He stood over him and watched him die. He wiped the knife on the *hombre's* shirt and proudly said, "Well, that package has no return on it."

Styx was jealous and a little torqued off because he hadn't killed the first one, that his cousin had the first kill. "Okay guys, let's get the money then we'll take care of the packages, if that's alright with you," which wasn't really a question but just Styx telling the cousin that he was still in charge.

To which the cousin replied, "Okay, okay," as his brother and he moved toward the front door.

With all the customers tied up, Styx turned his attention to the employees. "You, manager mister, you get over to the vault. Now! And open it up or no one, I mean no one, comes out of here alive."

"But I can't open the door yet, it can't be opened until five. Five and not before," the manager said, trying to stall the desperados.

"You can't fool me because you're a moron. How'd you like that boys? I got that from Bugs Bunny, ad libbed it a little bit for you," Styx said, all proud of himself.

Styx got up in the manager's face. "You pull that key from around your neck and open up that vault or I'll get it myself and you'll die right here and now." Then Styx pulled out his knife and nicked the managers cheek. As the manager pulled out the key, Styx thought, *Right where Isis said it would be.*

When the vault was opened, the two cousins and Styx couldn't believe their eyes. Boxes and bags of money, with the dye packs next to them. The employees wouldn't get a chance to use them now! "Okay boys, get them bags loaded," Styx demanded.

As they were loading the bags, there was a commotion that sounded like it came from the front door area. ...

CHAPTER TWENTY-FOUR

J.E.T. SLOWLY RODE BY THE bank, with the Deuce barely loping along. There was no one in the van, but there was a young woman in the back seat of that cherry red Impala SS. J.E.T. was thinking, *The car is running but she's in the back seat. Why?* He looked up at the bank's big glass window as he went by. Nothing, absolutely nothing could he see, except the reflection of that Western sky, which still looked like it was in the middle of an explosion. Then he felt like darkness was coming over the town and he wasn't thinking it was because it was beginning to be dusk.

J.E.T. turned off the ignition and the beast coasted to its parking spot. He dropped the kickstand, put that harnessed boot on the pavement and swung his other leg over the bike, never taking his eyes off the bank's front window or door. It felt like the calm before the storm.

When he stepped onto the sidewalk, J.E.T. scanned the area again. He saw a clearer view of the van's interior. Also of the SS, with only the girl in the back seat trying not to look at him. No one else was around. He slowly walked up to the front door, when the earth began to rumble and there was that familiar and dreadful sound of spurs. Then he felt like grandpa J.E.D. was with him. As Yogi would say, "deja vu all over again."

J.E.T. grabbed the door handle and suddenly saw through the glass a little girl standing about six feet back from the door, looking right at him. She looked emotionless—no smile, no frown, no nothing, just standing there looking at him.

J E.T. paused for just a second, wondering where she had emerged from. He pulled the door open. The glare caught his eyes for a split second and then she was gone, but to where?

Now the girl wasn't there, but two bruisers big enough to give The Rock a run for his money were standing there instead. One of them told J.E.T., "We've closed a little early today, see you tomorrow."

These guys were wearing flannels and jeans on a Thursday. *Yeah, I don't think they work here, 'cause no one ever said "casual Thursdays,"* J.E.T. thought. *Strange, they both have bandanas around their necks as well.*

J.E.T. looked them one by one in the eyes. On the wall just past the one to his right he could see the reflection of the lobby in a glass door. What he saw, folks lying on the floor, really didn't startle him because he had been given the warning. The two big dudes saw it in his eyes, that he knew.

Right then the two behemoths stepped toward J.E.T. As the one on his left came with a roundhouse punch that came all the way from New Mexico, the one on his right took the step to set up for a roundhouse kick that was coming from Yuma.

Time instantly slowed down for J.E.T. He knew he wasn't going to be able to stop this huge right hand, so he threw his left hand up and took a step back with his right foot.

Now he was out of the way of the punch and the kick. J.E.T.'s hand connected at the big boy's wrist and he let it go on by, to the bad boy's dismay.

J.E.T. then followed up by rotating his left hand and placing it on the elbow of the arm the bad boy had just tried to punch him with. Big Boy felt like he was stuck. He couldn't move his feet or his right arm and he couldn't reach J.E.T. with his left fist because J.E.T.'s left hand was holding the big boy's elbow against his body. He couldn't move for a few moments, but that was all J.E.T. needed.

J.E.T. had no choice and it came without him even thinking, but his right hand thrust like a spear right into the big boy's liver and then into his carotid artery. This stopped the flow of blood to the right side of his brain. The big boy fell right there.

Sorry, Sifu. I know that thrusting hands don't go out the school door, but this is that one occasion.

Big boy number one dropped like a "pop fly in the sun." Now it was time to deal with number two bad guy.

For a big guy he had some fast hands and feet, so he must have done some training along the way. First response after the failed kick and his cousin getting dropped was a straight punch that was deflected by J.E.T.'s right palm strike. This turned out just like he had hoped. The palm strike caused the big guy to spin around and with it came the spinning back kick. J.E.T. was thinking, *Please, you gonna to try that here, now?* With reflexes that number two didn't expect, J.E.T. kicked where the hamstring meets the glutes, taking him to his knees. This didn't feel good and totally surprised Big Boy. J.E.T. finished up with a palm strike to the base of the skull. The big boy fell onto his face and didn't move again.

If this didn't separate the skull from his spine, he would wake up with a perpetual headache. With both big boy one and big boy two down, J.E.T. set his sights on the others. How many more, he was about to find out.

While his cousins were getting pummeled at the front door, Styx was in the vault amid his greed and lust for the money that he claimed was his, knowing full well that it wasn't. Styx had packed up about five of the bags when he finally realized his cousin was calling him.

"Styx get out here, they just got beat down," Case yelled, referring to one and two cousins.

"What?" Styx questioned.

"Get out here," Case said again.

As Styx looked out of the vault, Case opened fire on J.E.T. When he did, one of the other big boys, who had initially been upstairs, came out of the vault and started shooting as well.

J.E.T. had jumped back near the front door, behind the cover of the corner there. So far, the bullets weren't penetrating the wall. J E.T. was thinking, *This wood is so old it's like iron now.*

He was also thinking, *This is a hornet's nest, but I'm the d-CON to handle it.*

J.E.T. still had the door-window mirror to tell him what was going on in the lobby. But he couldn't see the vault area. That was where the rounds were coming from now. If he wanted to see that area, he would have to stick his head out just a little bit. But would that little bit be too much?

"I don't know who you are, but if you want to live, you better go back out that front door!" Styx yelled, thinking he could scare J.E.T. away. "This wheel gun is going to wheel you right into Hell if you don't leave!"

"I can't leave when you've invited me to your party; that would be rude of me," J.E.T. yelled back. "And oh, by the way, I'm a deputy U.S. Marshal. So now you've just invited yourself to my party. You just checked yourself in."

The bullets stopped flying long enough to get their introductions taken care of.

"Hey," J.E.T. yelled, "My name is Taylor but folks call me J.E.T. What's your name?"

"You don't need to know my name. You just need to leave," Styx replied, still trying to buffalo J.E.T.

"Well, kid, that's *no bueno*. You know I can't do that. What's your name?" J.E.T. said, trying to get Styx to open up.

Styx got the other two cousins to take the bags of money to the side door where Carhop was. He told them to do it when the gunfire started back up. When the cousins got through the door, the shooting stopped again.

The cousins got the bags out to the van and the car. But before they came back in, Isis got out of the car and confronted them.

"What's going on in there, why are you shooting?" she asked the cousins. She was scared and didn't want any of her "friends" to get hurt.

"Isis get back in the car, none of this concerns you now," one of the big cousins told her.

"I'm not. I'm not getting back in that car!" she replied.

"Get back in that car," he told her again. This time she just walked away.

"This is not how this was supposed to go down," Isis said as she walked down the street.

"Hey, brother, let's get back in there. We got some killing to do," big boy number three said gleefully. "Leave her be. That's just more money for us."

"Carhop, let us in," Big Boy said. Carhop had ducked down under a desk. He didn't want to come out.

"Carhop, you better let us in," he said again, as Carhop duck walked over to the door and let them in.

On the way in, one of the cousins backhanded Carhop and told him, "Don't make me tell you twice again," as a welt started raising on Carhop's cheek.

"Okay, okay," Carhop responded, rubbing his cheek.

J.E.T. had returned fire a few times, but was conserving rounds as much as possible since he only had about thirteen rounds with him. As he tried to pie the corner, he knew he needed to return a few rounds because he couldn't stay in that position much longer. Then a hail of bullets came his way. This time they ripped through the corner of the wall. Just like darts, splinters of wood came ripping through J.E.T.'s left deltoid. A pencil-sized splinter went through his left thigh as well.

J.E.T. looked himself over and felt the wounds, thinking, *Well, at least the shoulder doesn't appear to have much bleeding. That's good. Let's check out the leg.*

As J.E.T. was trying to determine the damage to his leg, he thought, *That splinter is about the size of a number two pencil. Feels like a number three and a half though,* as he chuckled through the pain. *That's awfully close to the femoral artery. If it is, I have, maybe, thirty seconds.*

After assessing his injuries, J.E.T. was quite surprised that there was hardly any blood coming out of his wounds. *Must have missed that artery "by that much."* He was thinking of a fraction of an inch. *Well, if it's good enough for Maxwell Smart, then it's good enough for me!*

I have got to try to lure these guys out, now that my ammo is almost dry, J.E.T. thought, *plus bad guy number one and bad guy number two. I've used their ammo too. If they hadn't used the clerks and civilians for cover then I might have been able to get some of them.*

"Hey, kid! Do you realize you got what you asked for?" J.E.T. yelled between bullets flying. "By the way, what's your name?"

"Well since you haven't got much longer, Marshal, it's Del Rio!!" Styx stated very proudly.

"Del Rio! Kid, it was me who went to Muskogee to pick you up on Con-Air. And now you fall into my lap. Oh, and by the way, it was me that you almost hit on the side of the road near Coweta in the rain," J.E.T. said matter-of-factly.

"You know, Marshal, I punched my driver because he didn't run you over. I guess it was meant to be anyway, that I kill you here in Arizona instead of Oklahoma," Styx bragged. "Hey kid, be careful what you wish for. You just might get it." J.E.T. responded. "By the way kid, you might as well give up while you're behind."

"You mean ahead, don't you?" Styx came back.

"Please. By the way, Del Rio, you're just window dressing." J.E.T. felt like throwing that in there, just to get under Del Rio's skin.

"What do you mean, 'window dressing?'" Styx asked as he got more angsty by the moment.

"Well, Del Rio, it means all show and no go. No offense, 'cause I know you're trying hard to be hard for your boys here," J.E.T. said, getting him riled up and thinking, *Any time now, Del Rio's gonna make a mistake, any minute.* "By the way, what is y'all's name, The Mild Bunch?" This really made Del Rio even more angry.

"Del Rio, where did your boy go over by the side door?" J.E.T. asked, knowing that Carhop had found a hiding place under some desk so he wouldn't get shot. J.E.T. knew this kaleidoscope of a crew would look that way and he could get into a better position to take out another one of the big boys.

While Styx was yelling at Carhop to quit being a wuss, J.E.T. was able to work his way to some cabinets near the clerk's windows without being seen. The big boy who was guarding the customers now didn't see J.E.T.'s stealthy move. He as well had momentarily got fixated on Carhop, who was very craven at this time.

J.E.T. found another window for reflection at this position, so now he could see there were five of these pilferers. He held his finger to his lips so that the hostages wouldn't give away his position. Thankfully, they complied, some between tears and sobbing, but they complied.

With only a few rounds left, he knew he could take out the next one that got close enough for him to grab, like he did years ago on the rez when he broke through the door and put the habeas grabbus on the dad with a gun.

The big boy number three tried to sneak over to J.E.T.'s position near the door by swinging wide and getting close to the cabinets.

Too late! J.E.T.'s harnessed boot came across Big Dude's head so fast and hard that it felt like a lightning bolt had just struck him.

J.E.T. pulled that right foot back into position and, just as fast, gave the dude another kick, this time in the floating ribs. *Yeah, that rib's going to puncture something,* J.E.T. thought as he heard a huge gasp for air and the big boy spun around down to the floor. *Whoa, was that a triple lutz?* J.E.T. asked himself, with a big grin on his face.

"Hey Del Rio," J.E.T. yelled, rednecking him a little more. "You know your odds are dwindling by the minute, don't you? That big thud that you just heard, that was big boy number three. I see there are four of you left. This heist of the century is kind of losing it sizzle."

"What the ... ? Shut up, Marshal!" Styx yelled, getting really torqued off now because he had lost three of his big cousins and all of a sudden, things started looking a little bleak. He knew he needed to get out of there fast.

"Marshal, this is going to burst your bubble. I know you don't have much ammo left, so here's the plan. We're leaving and you're staying," Styx hollered, feeling good about his new plan.

"Case, you and cuz grab these three bags of money and head toward the side door. Make Carhop carry one of the bags," Styx directed his crew. "I'm going to lay down cover fire for you guys. But wait at the door and lay down fire for me to keep this deputy off our backs."

The rounds started coming J.E.T.'s way again, but the cabinets were doing a good job of not letting any of the bullets through. First rounds came from behind the clerk's counter, then they started flying from the side door area.

J.E.T. got off a few courtesy rounds between this hail of gunfire, but he just couldn't get into a good position to get off a good shot.

Just then, J.E.T. heard screams along with the gunfire. They were shooting the hostages lying on the floor. Then the shooting stopped as the side door shut.

J.E.T. popped his head up from behind the cabinet, scanned the carnage that lay before him and saw they were all gone.

Crying, sobbing and screaming came from the customers. J.E.T. grabbed belts, packing tape, electrical cords. He ripped shirts and made bandages. It was about five minutes of intensity, trying to keep these people alive.

CHAPTER TWENTY-FIVE

WHIT HAD BEEN IN THE diner waiting for J.E.T. to come back from the bank. The wind had whipped up and had been howling and whistling through the town for fifteen minutes or so, masking any sound in that area. As the wind calmed down, Whit heard what sounded like a barrage of gunfire. He jumped up and out the diner he went. Kari Ann tried to stop him but he wasn't having it. His little brother might be in trouble and there was no stopping him.

The signs of Huntington's were prevalent now. There was no running for Whit anymore. But the courage to fight this disease was even more prevalent.

As he was making his way to the bank, coming up on the van he saw two men approaching, each with a big bag in his hand. He also noticed two more young men behind these two. Same thing—a bag with each of them also.

"Hey, you two fellers seen a guy about forty years old or so, six feet one inch. with a black vest on?" Whit asked big boy number four.

"Yeah," big boy number four said as he looked back toward the bank. "I think I saw him back there," Big Boy said as he dropped the money bag with a classic look back. "You need to leave now or I'm gonna kick your tail," big boy told Whit.

Whit's quick response, which he has always had, was, "Well, you just did the easy part; you talked about it. So step aside boys, this is for grownups!"

This, Big Boy thought as he took a half step back, *is a perfect setup for the ol' one-two combination.*

Little did Big Boy know that Whit had been training in martial arts for thirty years, even in his physically depleted condition. First there was

Wing Chun, then Jeet Kune Do, then some Tai Chi with a side of Kung Fu San Soo. Don't forget a little Karate and some Kenpo for dessert. He was truly a mixed martial artist. A true martial artist!!

If there was one thing Whit loved to do back in the day, it was spar and fight. He didn't care what martial arts style, or his opponent's size or age.

When that first punch came, Whit's reflexes, strength, speed and knowledge came back to him like he was a prime thirty-year-old man again.

First block of the right hook came with a palm strike with his right hand. Then a block with an edge hand, also with his right hand. But Whit let that hand come through because bad boy number four was such a big strong feller.

Whit followed up that block with a sidekick to the inner part of Big Boy's right thigh. When Whit brought his left leg back, he turned it into a sweep of Big Boy's left leg and at the same time he gave him a palm strike to the face.

This took Big Boy down so fast that his head bounced off of the sidewalk. Then Whit obliged him with a stomp to the junk!

"Next," Whit calmly said to Case as he tried to get there before his cousin took a beating. Too late!

A straight kick came Whit's way. Poor guy's brain didn't register in time that big boy number four had just taken a beating.

Case tried to kick Whit, but Whit's reflexes were so fast that he was able to take a half step back with his left foot and gave a palm strike to Case's shin. At the same time came a toe kick that split the hamstring of the leg that Case had just tried to kick with.

While Case was kicking, he had also thrown a straight punch. When Whit brought his foot back from his counter kick, it went automatically to a side kick. Not only this but Whit blocked the punch and as he side kicked Case, he had a hold of Case's arm. Case's upper body took all of the force of the kick since Whit didn't let go of his arm.

Then Whit proceeded to keep ahold of Case's right arm, where he switched hands and held Case's right arm with his left hand. When his right hand came off of the block, it struck Case in the upper lip with a side palm. Oh, what a pressure point to hit someone at.

This absolutely stunned Case, but now came the good part for Whit. The flurry of roll punches that Whit applied to Case was a thing of beauty. He followed Case's face all the way to the ground with those punches.

Then Whit's signature move, a stomp to the junk. Case definitely wasn't getting up anytime soon.

CHAPTER TWENTY-SIX

"SPEED ON BROTHER, HELL AIN'T half full," Styx quietly said.

"What?" Carhop asked.

"Just reading a bumper sticker out loud. It's nothing," Styx said, pondering....

Whit cautiously went into the bank, wondering what kind of mess he was about to see.

"Bro', come here," a familiar voice said. J.E.T. was so happy to see Whit. "Hey, give me some help here patching these folks up."

"Deputy, you all right?" Whit asked, seeing J.E.T.'s shoulder and thigh torn up.

"Yeah, I'm good," J.E.T. said. "Whit, did you see four dudes out front of the bank, maybe with duffle bags?" J.E.T. asked.

"Yeah, I did. Two of them are on the sidewalk and two of them left in an Impala SS," Whit responded.

"Dadgummit, Bro'! I need to get them thugs. Can you take care of these folks—I got them all except this one—while I go get these last two criminals?" J.E.T. asked. "Oh, and can I get your car keys, just in case that SS is souped up? They have between a five- and ten-minute start on me."

"No problemo. I got this here. You go get them bad *hombres*. And you're going to have to drive it like you stole it," Whit told his little brother. "I bet that's the last time they do drive-thru banking," Whit thought to himself but said out loud.

"I'll call 911 on my way out," J.E.T hollered as he was leaving.

J.E.T. ran by the two guys that Whit had taken out. They were not going to get up anytime soon. *So, I see you met Whit,* J.E.T. chuckled to himself on his way to the diner, and jumped into the Black Z.

Whit had told J.E.T. that the SS went south, so he figured that was the fastest way to the highway. When he fired up that '69 Z, a familiar guitar and the voice of Jimi was on the radio: "There must be some way out of here, said the joker to the thief." J.E.T. just kinda thought, *how apropos.*

As J.E.T. pulled out, that first gear saw the Z drifting and J.E.T. was thinking, *Like I was sixteen again, when I was drifting before drifting was cool.*

Then when he hit second gear his mind thought, *NOTHING,* third gear, *BUT,* fourth gear, *SCREAM!!!*

Before he knew it, the Z28 was going three miles a minute!!! He knew he could catch the Impala SS whether it was hopped up or not. But he thought he could sure use a javelina to get in that car's way out here in this open desert.

CHAPTER TWENTY-SEVEN

BEFORE ZAR AND REGA COULD get a half block away from the diner, a platoon of ghouls was going to head them off, or at least try, because these ghouls didn't want anyone or anything stopping their bad boys' intentions.

The leader of this bunch was none other than Recon Rage. He had caused so much destruction throughout the ages with all the seditious actions he'd instigated.

As Recon Rage and ZAR came face to face, Recon Rage pulled out both of his swords and got ZAR's response: "Oh, you have two swords; that's cute!!" ZAR then pulled his sword and the battle was on, with ZAR and REGA against Recon Rage and his platoon of no-gooders.

At this point in the fight, ZAR had seen many different platoons. There was Doubt, there was Greed, there was Vanity, there was a Drug and Alcohol Intoxication platoon. You name it, they were there.

ZAR saw an old foe. "Hey, Dope."

The demon responded, "It's Weed to you, ZAR."

ZAR, rednecking the demon, responded to the ghoul, "Well, it was Dope, then Grass, then Weed. I don't know you anymore, but I do know that smell!"

The Prince of Southern Arizona was having his way with the Styx bunch. He was directing his minions at them, and especially toward Styx.

Recon Rage's platoon was making it very difficult for ZAR and REGA to fight through when J.E.T. had already made it to the front door of the bank.

ZAR had taken a few glances into the bank and knew he needed to give J.E.T. his warning. ZAR spun back down to the ground, pulled his arms to his side, raised his chin and gave the deepest growl he'd had to give J.E.T., ever!!

The ground rumbled and J.E.T.'s spurs jingled. ZAR saw that little girl in the front of the bank's door that J.E.T. was about to enter. J.E.T. didn't know that this was no little girl. This was a demon who was fully there, but J.E.T. could only see a little girl.

ZAR saw that REGA was closer than he was to that demon and he made a signal to REGA to take out that demon's setup.

ZAR, with his mighty force and sword, took out the front line of the platoon, leaving just enough room for REGA to react. REGA saw in J.E.T.'s eyes that he was wondering, *Where did this girl come from?* And at just the split second when J.E.T. pulled the door open, REGA hit the demon broadside and sent him out the other side of the bank.

The "rage" goon squad summoned another platoon. They arrived to help against ZAR and REGA.

During this fight against the barbarians, ZAR could see through the melee that J.E.T. was handling himself pretty well with the first two bruisers and had made quick order of them. But right now, he and REGA just couldn't get to him because REGA had been swarmed after he took out the little girl demon.

There were swords flying, and there were punches and kicks flying as well. But right now, the fiery darts were attacking J.E.T. and his shield of faith was sure taking a beating. But all of the scriptures he had read and absorbed throughout his life were keeping that shield strong.

Also, the physical training he had done since he was a young boy was paying dividends, whether it was when he was going to work in construction at eleven years old with his dad and brother, or the Kung Fu training that started when he was ten and the Aikido training when he was seventeen. Then there was the weight training that started when he was about twenty-two years old. All of this added up to a strong shield of faith.

There were a few openings that let ZAR send some of his angelic feathers J.E.T.'s way. There were some awfully big darts, more like arrows and spears, that the demons of Doubt and Confusion were sending towards J.E.T. "Okay, Doubt, you didn't really think you were going to get to J.E.T. did you?" ZAR rednecked the ghoul. With the speed and precision of a flick of ZAR's wings, ZAR would intercept these major fiery darts before they could get to J.E.T. because if they weren't deflected, J.E.T. might have become too discouraged to continue the fight.

Just then, ZAR could sense it coming. He wasn't going to be able to stop the bullets or guide them to miss J.E.T. TWO HITS!!

ZAR knew there is a purpose when this happens and that he would still do everything he possibly could. Sometimes he could do more and sometimes he wasn't allowed to continue in the fight.

At that moment, ZAR sent two of his feathers into J.E.T.'s wounds. Injury to his thigh was significant because it was close to the femoral artery. For now, he knew the bleeding in J.E.T.'s shoulder would stop and would slow to barely trickle in his thigh, but he thought, *For how long?*

ZAR didn't seem to worry about J.E.T.'s pain threshold because J.E.T. had so much adrenaline running through him at that moment. Yeah, J.E.T. felt a major sting but not the severe damage that it had caused.

Right now, there were several more platoons sent ZAR and REGA's way. Just when they were battling and had got within fifty feet of the bank, these extra tormentors joined the fight.

With AILIN, ROBATO and ASTRAL not being able to get in this battle, ZAR and REGA could not break free and get through to their squires.

The other three angels were picking up skirmishes at the diner. Right now it was three angels with four squires, since REGA was deep in battle with ZAR.

ZAR saw the firefight in the bank. The same way the bullets had missed Captain Washington, before he became President, was how he was stopping them from hitting J.E.T. The flick of his wings sent feathers J.E.T.'s way, blocking the fatal bullets' path. Except for those two rounds!!

ZAR briefly saw J.E.T.'s next close-quarters combat when he quickly dispatched number three big guy. "That's it, *compadre*," ZAR said, smiling as his sword was doing damage the hellions didn't expect.

The carnage that ZAR and REGA had left all around them was unimaginable—so many of the demonic foes strewn about. But it didn't even look like they had made a dent in the "rage."

More platoons were sent their way. It seemed endless. With the Son giving these angelic phenoms their strength, speed and stamina, there was no letup.

Then came a long-time foe. The spirit of Pride showed up to the "rage," in what he thought was all his glory. He had at least three platoons with him, and their false bravado.

When he started coming in ZAR's direction, ZAR said, "You're looking a little ashy," knowing that dig would get under Pride's skin, especially considering how awesome he thought he was. "Oh, I know why. You haven't been near the Son to give you that beautiful glow you once had." Just a little extra zing from ZAR.

ZAR was fighting these powers and principalities alongside REGA, but they couldn't get to the bank with the all those demons pouring in, into and out of Styx and his desperado crew.

All of a sudden, ZAR saw the hail of gunfire that was headed in J.E.T.'s direction. He somehow got REGA's attention and they both defended J.E.T. with their feathers. Thankfully, not one bullet hit J.E.T. in this barrage of gunfire. Now J.E.T. was left in the bank helping the customers and the bad guys had taken the money and run.

"Make way, Guardians," ASTRAL said proudly, "my squire is coming through. Now's your time, warrior, now's your time!!" Even with the Sea of Doubt demons trying to get to Whit, they couldn't penetrate his armor or get past ASTRAL.

ASTRAL saw that the Good Lord had given back all of Whit's speed, strength and knowledge to where it was like he was thirty years old again.

ASTRAL was now in the battle with ZAR and REGA, taking on these legions, much to his delight.

"Brothers, do you see what Whit is doing to those empty souls?" ASTRAL asked the two angels with excitement in his voice, seeing Whit physically, mentally and emotionally like he once was. "Those two heathens didn't have time to tap out; Whit just gave them the knockout," ASTRAL said to whoever was listening.

There came a new wave of beasts the three nobles had to contend with. J.E.T. and Whit were out of the Guardians' range because the Guardians hadn't been able to penetrate that rogue blockade.

ZAR and ASTRAL saw that Whit had made it into the bank after his little bad guy's beat down and was helping J.E.T. for now.

As Styx and Carhop were leaving, most of the demonic realm stayed there to keep the Guardians from following Styx.

ZAR saw that J.E.T. had gotten Whit's keys, was running down the block, and was leaving in the Z. But ZAR was unable to follow him because this fight was a long way from over.

ZAR briefly remembered when he fought the Prince of Persia and was delayed for three weeks in giving Daniel his answer from God. ZAR wondered how long would this battle take, when would he, REGA and ASTRAL get back to their men, and would he have to call MICHAEL to get past these denomics?

CHAPTER TWENTY-EIGHT

THEY WENT DOWN THE HIGHWAY with the speedometer pegged. "Boy, you can drive!" Styx said as he was looking through the back window, watching the town get smaller and smaller, although nothing was fast enough for this chronic felon when he was going down the methamphetamine raceway. As they neared Highway 79, he said, "Go south on 79, like we planned. Those boys can catch up with us when we get to Tucson's meeting place."

"Do you think any of the others made it? Our boys were scattered in the bank and outside on the sidewalk," Carhop said. He seemed a little worried about the rest of the gang, with his foot mashed on the throttle, going a hundred and thirty plus miles an hour!

"If they don't get here, we'll split this money. It will take us a long way," Styx responded, but not very convincingly.

Carhop was thinking, *Am I going to be the next one lying on the ground?* while trying to get through the confusion of the bank shootout and losing his boys.

When they'd already gone twenty to twenty-two miles, Styx saw headlights that had come out of nowhere. And they were getting brighter.

"Carhop, there's someone behind us and their lights are getting bigger," Styx said, with worry in his voice.

"No way!" Carhop said, surprised and in disbelief. "This car's fast and there's just no way that anyone could gain on us."

As J.E.T. was just past the outskirts of town, he was hitting the apexes and hitting those curves late and deep. This brought back memories of the Indian Police Academy and how he had tied for fastest lap on the road course—most fun part of the whole academy, hands down.

After five or six minutes on the road, J.E.T. saw some small red lights in the distance. *It's that dirty duo,* he thought. *Keep your line and find out.*

If that was a regular car I would have caught him by now, so I'm thinking that must be the Impala SS with the dos muy mal hombres! J.E.T. thought, with his hands tightly gripping the steering wheel.

"You're going to need a Z/29 and a half if you want to outrun this black beauty. 'Cause this is the beauty and the beast all rolled up into one," J.E.T. said out loud, smiling and turning up Hendrix's lead a few decibels higher than the engine roar.

Not much longer and they'll be in my sights, J.E.T. thought, anticipating and going through more scenarios in his mind.

ZAR and REGA's battle was non-stop, with the flaming darts, arrows, swords and spears.

ZAR had sent so many fireballs the demons' way that his sword was glowing red hot. But these two still weren't making a dent; it just kept the demons off of them. It was all swords, fists, feet and fireballs from ZAR.

REGA had his own weapons of choice and they never stopped either.

ASTRAL had gotten to Whit and put him in his cocoon, not letting anyone from the dark world get to him. Even though they wanted Whit, they wanted J.E.T. and ZAR even more.

The legions of Gloom and Doom had arrived and joined in the battle. The skies were almost black from the throng of goblins sent this way. All of the top players came to inhabit Styx and to do battle with his enemies. But they didn't expect ZAR and four of the Angelic Secret Service.

The fight was now going on thirty minutes and J.E.T. was going over the horizon, out of ZAR's view. But this fight wasn't even close to being over. Right now there was no exit strategy—just fight until there's an opening to get to J.E.T. and trust J.E.T.'s skills and instincts to get him through until ZAR could get there. He wondered if his feathers would continue to stop J.E.T.'s bleeding.

CHAPTER TWENTY-NINE

"WATCH IT!!" STYX YELLED AS a javelina crossed the road.

At 135 miles an hour there is nothing anyone can do. The SS took a big hit and it was all Carhop could do to keep it on all four wheels.

The thud was almost deafening. The impact was so jolting it knocked the breath out of them both and the spinning made them dizzy. That car was "tore up!"

After the screeching and the car ending up with the driver-side front tire on the pavement, the rest of the car was on an angle in the dirt, off of the shoulder of the highway.

The car was now facing the way it had come. With dust and dirt still flying and only one headlight working, these thugs were in a world of disorientation, along with some bruising and a lack of oxygen in their lungs.

Carhop was able to get himself out of the car first. "Styx, Styx, you all right?" he called.

"Yeah, I'm all right. Why'd you hit that pig?" Styx asked, knowing that it couldn't be avoided. "Get this door open. Those headlights are getting closer and closer!"

Carhop got the car door open and pulled Styx out. Styx gave Carhop orders to get across the road, just in case this was the law or, even worse, Deputy Marshal Taylor.

"If it's Taylor or whoever, we'll have to ambush them. Now get over there and don't be a chicken!" Styx yelled. "Now give me your gun!"

"I don't have it and I don't know where it went. I must have lost it when we hit that javelina," Carhop responded, still feeling a little shook up and perturbed at Styx.

"I don't have mine either, but I do have this knife," Styx said with a devilish grin on his face, as he pulled it out of its sheath.

"He's almost here. Now get over there," Styx yelled.

J.E.T. saw all lights disappear and then all of a sudden a headlight appeared out of nowhere, even though the lights were maybe five or six miles ahead.

What's this? J.E.T. thought. *Is that a motorcycle? Where'd the taillights go? Well, whatever it is, I'll be there in a minute and a half or two.*

As J.E.T. hit that last apex on the turn in the road, before he got to Styx and Carhop, he could tell it was a car with one headlight out because both parking lights were still working.

J.E.T. started slowing down about a mile from the criminals. He needed to get close enough to use his headlights, but not too close because it might be a trap, a setup.

J.E.T. zigzagged, trying to look down both sides of the road. Nothing was on the right-hand side but some sagebrush. On the left side of the road, he couldn't see what was on the other side of the spun-out SS. But now he knew he had the hooligans. And this time they were not getting away.

He turned off the headlights so as not to get silhouetted by his own lights.

As ZAR was in the fight with Pride, he asked, "What's so special about this kid that you are pulling out all stops? 'Cause from what I see, he ain't nothing special, just another lackey."

Pride was still butt hurt from ZAR earlier in the battle so he wouldn't answer him. He was acting like a three-year-old but was still giving a good fight. Like all bangers, he was not demon enough to go *mano a mano* into the fight; they always have to fight unfair.

ZAR actually preferred fighting multiple assailants. But this was a little excessive because we're talking many thousands that he and REGA were fighting, along with the other three. Those three were getting some licks in every so often as well, when a stray occasionally came their way or when ASTRAL followed Whit into the midst of chaos.

That chase of J.E.T.'s had taken him to the horizon. Mostly, ZAR was now only hearing him. Between the blackness of the population of demons and J.E.T.'s distance, ZAR heard that Z28's rpm fall from about 7700 down to idle. Then the ignition was turned off.

J.E.T., hang in there brother. Now's the time to go all Chief Attakullakulla on them two empties, ZAR thought. *You got the bloodline of J.E.D. and Chief Attakullakulla, who got his name Warrior from actually being a warrior. The Chief was fighting with the war parties up until his late fifties. He was a thrill to watch—small in stature but he fought like he was six feet four.*

CHAPTER THIRTY

J.E.T. PULLED HIMSELF OUT OF the '69, his hands a little stiff and body a little tense. That was the first time he'd driven anything that could go 180 miles per hour and stay at that speed for twenty to twenty-five minutes, although he didn't need that much time. He just barely pushed the door closed without latching it, trying not to make any sound that would give him away.

J.E.T. had no ammo left from that firefight at the bank, just his trusty stiletto. He was sure hoping they didn't have any ammo either.

J.E.T. stopped for a few moments, just to listen, listen for anything—rocks moving, heavy breaths, bushes rustling, anything—before he would go check out the car.

Then a slight grin came across his face. *Huh, a javelina,* he thought as he saw it lying there on the side of the road. He chuckled to himself.

Styx knew J.E.T. was coming his way. Since he was behind the car, he threw a small pebble to the other side of the road, just before J.E.T. got to him.

When the pebble hit the dirt on the other side of the road, J.E.T.'s head snapped toward the sound.

The few steps J.E.T. took toward the pebble was all Styx needed. He jumped from behind the car and with an overhand strike came down with his knife. J.E.T. sensed it coming but not in time. It hit J.E.T. in the same shoulder he'd been shot in, but it was not a solid blow.

Before J.E.T. could get his knife out of his pocket, again he sensed something or someone coming up behind him from the other side.

A half step back with his right foot and an arcing right hand to clear whatever was coming his direction. He had stepped out of the way of an overhand strike of a cane-sized stick from Carhop, who had been hiding among the sagebrush. This clearing motion caused the stick to hit Carhop in the shin and man, did it smart!

Simultaneously with this clearing, J.E.T. had to return his attention back to Styx, who was getting ready to take another slice of him.

With a well-timed sidekick, even in the dark, J.E.T. connected to Styx in the lower abdomen. This caught Styx off guard and not only drove him back, but stunned him for a few moments.

Now J.E.T. turned his attention back to Carhop, who was in the beginning of a baseball swing. J.E.T. stepped into Carhop before he could generate any power. This stopped his arms from swinging. With Carhop's arms trapped, now came a crushing blow from an elbow, after which came a simultaneous palm strike to the face and a leg sweep.

It almost felt like one hit, the elbow strike, the palm strike, the leg sweep and then Carhop hitting the ground. His head and the ground became one. Carhop lay there stunned and dazed, but he got up after a few moments because he knew that if he didn't, Styx would probably kill him if he got ahold of him. So he picked himself up.

J.E.T. turned his attention back to Styx, and none too soon. That last kick of J.E.T.'s had sent Styx into the light of the Impala.

With a flash of the steel in Styx's hand came the uppercut. Styx was trying to gut J.E.T. But even with the injuries he had received, J.E.T. was too fast to take a solid blow.

Just when J.E.T. reacted with the back of his forearm, to make sure no vital arteries were hit, along came another swing from Carhop.

J.E.T. guided Styx's right arm into the hand of Carhop that was holding the stick. And now J.E.T. was facing Carhop. So he obliged Carhop with a kick to the stomach. Carhop got the double—a bad cut on his hand and a sweet kick to the bread basket.

J.E.T. followed this kick with a left-hand block that replaced the right-hand block of the knife. Well, that right hand now followed Styx's arm right to the part of the upper lip just under the nose. This edge hand strike sent a few tears out of Styx's eyes. They always do!

Carhop had taken a pretty good beating along with Styx, but those two "greasers" from Tulsa were pretty tough. They were tough enough to be "carnies" for sure.

Carhop got up again. Every blow he took was getting magnified but he was going to give it one more shot.

J.E.T. was thinking, *I have to end this fast,* as he noticed the blood starting to almost become a stream going down his arm. *What's in my boot?* he thought. Well, the headlight revealed the story. The gunshot wound on his leg from the bank had opened up pretty good and was forming a puddle of blood in his boot.

Carhop came at J.E.T. with his head down a little and with his right arm held back like he was reaching from Tucson. *This is an invitation to get finished,* J.E.T. thought. He stepped forward with his left foot and put his left arm up to block the punch, but the punch never got there. J.E.T.'s right hand and fingers, shaped like a spear, thrust into the base of Carhop's neck just under his chin.

Then J.E.T. brought his right hand over Carhop's right arm and cleared it out of the way. With deadly speed and power, he brought his left hand back behind Carhop's head and, with a swift twist, struck the back of Carhop's skull. Carhop went down and there is no way he was going to get back up, ever.

J.E.T. spun around and, feeling his strength and stamina waning, looked for Styx. "Del Rio, all of these bad choices that you've made, don't make another one. Because you will get what you ask for and that's me," J.E.T. said, with a warning....

After the EMTs arrived at the bank, Whit went out to the big boy's van. *They don't need this anymore,* Whit thought. He left probably ten minutes or so after J.E.T. He had to head south and find his little brother.

He took off in the direction he had told J.E.T. to go, hoping to get there in time for a little beat-down action.

Going about eighty-five miles an hour was a snail's pace for him after owning that Z for so long. He said to himself, *Does this thing have a guv-na or is it just slow?*

Deputy, I know you got this, but just hang in there. He was praying and remembering the wounds to J.E.T.'s shoulder and thigh.

After about forty to forty-five minutes, he could see taillights and a headlight. And they didn't look like they were moving.

ZAR and his special forces were doing so much damage, the demons were dropping into great big piles.

ZAR said to a bunch coming his way, "Really? You're coming at me like a 'can of corn.' Next, not another weak ground ball. Oh, you want some chin music? Hey brothers, you want me to kick out some Yogisms now?"

The demons seemed a little confused by what ZAR was saying. That's when the special forces responded to ZAR. They formed a wedge and split through multitudes of demons because they knew he needed to get to J.E.T.

As ZAR was on his way, he caught the tail end of the beatdown J.E.T. had given Carhop and he could now hear J.E.T. giving Styx his final warning....

Styx took off running across the headlight of the SS and as he did, J.E.T. took off as well. J.E.T. didn't have time to go around the car so in mid stride, without thinking, he hurdled and broad-jumped the disabled car. While in midair, he thought about his old buddy back in Oklahoma who did this jump on a regular basis.

While he was clearing the car with a flying sidekick, he pulled out his stiletto. He wasn't about to let this criminal get away.

When J.E.T. landed, he slid to a stop in front of Styx. As Styx swung that big blade, J.E.T took a full step back and the blade missed. *High cheese,* J.E.T. thought as the knife just missed his throat. Just as quickly, J.E.T. took a full step forward and before Styx could bring the knife back around, J.E.T. delivered four fatal stabs: one to the femoral artery, one to the liver, one to the aorta and one to the carotid artery.

Styx didn't move another inch, except to fall to the ground, and he succumbed to his injuries within seconds.

J.E.T. stood there for a few seconds, just looking at this murderer, thinking of the lives that were lost and the lives that were saved. As he turned to go up the embankment, his legs gave way from under him and he fell to his knees. He just sat there in that kneeling position, losing strength by the moment. He thought, *So this is how it feels to lose your blood—cold and tired.*

Then his head dropped with his chin on his chest. Struggling to keep his eyes open, he just couldn't anymore.

"J.E.T! J.E.T! Bro', where are you?" Again, "J.E.T! J.E.T! Bro', where are you? Little brother!" Whit called but couldn't get an answer as he looked all over for his brother.

J.E.T. thought to himself, *I must be imagining this, but oh, how sweet Whit's voice sounds right now,* not knowing that his big brother was really there.

Whit looked to his right and then, when he looked back to his left, saw someone standing over him, looking down. Here was this huge angelic being, with eyes like flaming torches and arms and legs that looked like polished brass. This magnificent being knelt down beside J.E.T. and whispered to him, "Warrior, don't give up. Hang in there, brother." Then he raised J.E.T.'s chin and looked into his eyes.

Whit could see that even though those eyes were like flaming torches, they were full of love, love for his Lord and love for J.E.T.

ZAR picked up J.E.T. and told Whit, "Get the tape out of the glove box and wrap it around J.E.T.'s leg." Whit did, and then ZAR placed J.E.T. in the Z. When ZAR turned around, he put his hand on the back of Whit's neck and said in a whisper, because his voice is like thunder if he doesn't, "I can't tell you if he's going to make it, but you have to drive like you are seventeen again, and you can."

ZAR handed Whit the keys and just stood there, looking at J.E.T.

ASTRAL said, without looking at ZAR, "Your warrior is knockin' on heaven's door."

J.E.T. opened his eyes for a second. "You good, Bro'?" J.E.T. whispered as Whit was about to ignite the Z.

"Yeah, I'm good little brother, I'm good," Whit replied, with a tear in his eye.

"Okay Bro', as long as you're good, then I'm good. My best day ever!" Then J.E.T. rested his head on the window, shut his eyes and said quietly, "Thank you, Jesus."

When Whit fired up the Camaro, the radio hauntingly played Stevie Ray: "Oh now baby, tell me how have you been?" Whit just looked at the radio and said, "Life Without You," knowing that was J.E.T.'s favorite song.

Whit was hitting those gears and driving that 1969 Z/28 like he was seventeen!!

ZAR stood there gleaming like a lightning bolt, when all of a sudden he heard a roar coming up behind him in the distance, that familiar roar. When he looked over his massive shoulder, this Prince of Darkness and his riders were approaching in that cool Arizona air. ZAR looked back at the car blazing away, then raised his arms above his head, with his hands looking like they were grabbing the night sky, he spread his wings and let out a growl that sounded like thunder as he looked up to the heaven.

As Whit heard the thunder, he looked in the rearview mirror and a lightning bolt flashed across the sky!!!

THE GUARDIAN

First, I want to thank my Lord and Savior Jesus
Christ for giving me this story in a dream.

I also want to thank the three special women in my life:

My gorgeous wife, still gorgeous after twenty-five years,
My oldest daughter still perfect from the day she was born,
My youngest daughter, who reminds me of myself
(and no, she doesn't look like her mom!) What a
joy she is, so sweet, beautiful and funny.

To my posse, my brothers, my inspiration, my Guardians!*

*Kevin, I couldn't have asked for a better big brother. You
were always fearless in my eyes and so talented and funny.
*John, my oldest and dearest friend. The one with no
fear who brought this shy boy to the Lord at seven years
old, who stood in the way of many of my battles that
for whatever reason came my way. I can't think of when
you haven't been there for me when I needed you.
*Jr., who knew at eighteen and nineteen years old that we
would become so close? We moved to different states and took
the good times with the hard times. Those motorcycle trips
cemented our relationship for our lifetime. God is good.

*Bob, met you in the sixth grade. Always smiling and driven. Even with a bad heart, you always gave more than anyone would think possible. I probably wouldn't have made it through high school if it hadn't been for you and Alan. I love you and miss you, Bro'. I think about you quite often and it's been about ten years now since you've been gone.

*Alan, we met in the eighth grade. First it was the bikes that we had in common, then came the cars and girls, then our move to Oklahoma. Somewhere along the way we became brothers. The best though was when you gave your heart to the Lord.

*Ron, we forged our friendship in iron, literally! Those four years that we were partners at the gym were the best. I don't know where it happened, but when we thought we were just throwing the iron around we were actually forging our brotherhood.

*Kevin T., who would have thought that our families were friends from the '50s, that we would forge another friendship in the '80s? I always enjoyed working for you, but the friendship that we bonded into has meant so much more.

*Eddie, even though we were cousins, we didn't really know each other until we were twelve. But then that's when the brotherhood started. I have always been proud of you and what you have accomplished in your law enforcement career.

*Rick, I remember back when we were kids and teenagers, you being three years older than me. I never felt that you treated me like a little kid. Then when we became adults, it just seemed so effortless that our relationship turned from being cousins to brothers.

*Blake, what can I say? Friendship forged at the Sheriff's Office and at the gym. You could think outside the box—brave, funny and strong. Yeah, brothers.

*Denny, Donny and Darrin, growing up, it always felt like you were my and Kevin's cousins, and Big Denny and Gladys were more like an uncle and aunt to us. I am proud of how successful you three have become. A lot of years since you all were two, three and four years old, but when I see you all the friendship still feels the same.

*Julia, wow, I give you a few pictures and my thoughts of
how I wanted the cover to be and you did it "perfectly."
I knew you were the one to do this all along.
*Chris, thanks for your IT help, because I am so illiterate at IT.
*Bryan, thank you for your IT help as well.
*Ryan, thanks for your input. It was cool that
you knew the direction I was going.
*John S., my mentor from the SO, thanks for your help.
*Scott and Margie, thanks for the photo shoot, the cool 69
Z/28 and the cool gas station, it turned out like I had hoped.

I GREW UP A CONSTRUCTION worker and pastor's kid, moving throughout my childhood years between Oklahoma, Arizona, California and Utah. I was in construction myself from eleven years old until my early thirties, when I could no longer fight the draw of being in law enforcement. I got my start in law enforcement twenty-seven years ago, with the Cheyenne and Arapaho Tribes. So grateful and thankful for that opportunity. Best job of my life. The last twenty-three years have been with the Weld County Sheriff's Office. In my career I've been on patrol, worked in the jail and in the courts/transport unit (the second-best job of my life). I am a proud member of the Oklahoma Cherokee Nation and Irish. Kent Long